KENNY, COME HOME

When Jane Ross discovered that her younger brother, Kenny, had disappeared at the same time as his employer's safe had been robbed, she was horrified. Convinced that he was no thief, she was determined to learn the truth. By accepting a job in the garage where he worked and taking over his lodgings, both under an assumed name, Jane discovered that there was more to Kenny than she realised. And she was also surprised to learn that the outwardly aggressive garage owner, Doug Evans, was on her side after all.

SHEILA LEWIS

KENNY, COME HOME

Complete and Unabridged

LINFORD
Leicester

First published in Great Britain in 1983 by
Robert Hale Limited
London

First Linford Edition
published 1998
by arrangement with
Robert Hale Limited
London

Copyright © 1983 by Sheila Lewis
All rights reserved

British Library CIP Data

Lewis, Sheila
    Kenny, come home.—Large print ed.—
Linford romance library
    1. Love stories
    2. Large type books
    I. Title
823.9′14 [F]

ISBN 0–7089–5230–5

Published by
F. A. Thorpe (Publishing) Ltd.
Anstey, Leicestershire

Set by Words & Graphics Ltd.
Anstey, Leicestershire
Printed and bound in Great Britain by
T. J. International Ltd., Padstow, Cornwall

This book is printed on acid-free paper

1

"**B**UT why can't you come to Canada with us, Jane?" Emily Meade asked.

Jane Ross looked down at the small girl sitting beside her, and gently stroked her dark curls.

"Because I can't leave Kenny."

"Is he your brother?"

"Yes."

"Why doesn't he live with you like Tony lives with me?" Emily pointed to the three-year-old energetically digging in the children's sand pit.

Jane paused. "Well, Kenny's grown up and he didn't want to live in Ashburn." She looked beyond the garden of the Meade home at the small village half a mile away, with the rolling hills beyond it. It was so peaceful, so idyllic, she still found it difficult to understand Kenny's attitude. But then there was so little work in the country for a young twenty-year-old crazy about cars. And anyway, it had been for the best when he left.

"Where does he live then?" Emily piped up again.

"In Rowton — that's a big town about forty miles from here."

"Are there big towns in Canada, Jane?"

Jane was relieved that Emily had lost interest in Kenny. She didn't feel like talking any more about her brother. After all, she could hardly confide her worries to a six-year-old. And there was no doubt that she was worried about Kenny. But she knew there was nothing she could do about it until the Meades left for Canada the following day.

She answered Emily's questions not without some pangs of regret. If only she had heard from Kenny she might be going to Canada with the Meades. She had been nursery nurse to the family for the last two years and loved her job. She'd been so thrilled when she

2

heard the family was going to Canada. Harold Meade had unexpectedly been transferred to the Montreal branch of the business. The Meades had asked her to stay with them and while she knew her present job would only last until Tony was ready for school, the opportunity to spend a few years in Canada was very exciting.

And so she'd written to Kenny telling him of the chance and hoping he wouldn't mind. She intended saving most of her salary to make annual trips home. Kenny was her only relative, but it wasn't as if she was going for ever. And who knows, she might find more opportunities in Canada, not only for herself but also Kenny. Although they no longer shared a home, she was still very fond of her brother and hoped that one day they might be closer again. Perhaps she might find somewhere that afforded them both the opportunities and environment they wanted.

But he hadn't replied to her letter. There was only a Payphone at his digs

3

and that didn't take incoming calls so she hadn't been able to speak to him. He wasn't permitted personal calls at work either.

It was now three weeks since she'd written to Kenny — plenty of time for him to reply, particularly since she'd stressed how urgent things were. Mr Meade had been given no prior warning of his transfer.

But there was only silence from Kenny and she couldn't understand that. Surely if he'd intended taking a holiday he would have let her know? There was the possibility, of course, that he was ill — in hospital, even, but surely he would have let her know about that. She could have gone to Rowton to see him but she'd hesitated because every day she expected to hear from him.

Besides, there was so much to do at the Meade home, what with packing and taking the children to say goodbye to all their friends. And so the days had slipped by until she'd realised she could leave matters no longer. She had to tell the Meades she couldn't go to Canada and give them time to find a replacement for her. The new nurse was meeting the Meades at the airport next day.

★ ★ ★

Later, Jane made boiled eggs and toast soldiers for the children and they had tea together in the cosy nursery. She tried to keep everything bright and cheerful; there was no point in making it a sad occasion for the children, no matter how she felt.

After she'd put the children to bed she had her last chat with her employer, Sylvia Meade.

"There, Jane, glowing references," she handed an envelope to Jane. "And very well deserved too. Have you applied for a new post yet?"

"Not yet. I'll take a week or so off, I hope I can spend some time with Kenny, then come back to Ashburn."

She hadn't told Mrs Meade about Kenny's silence, only that she felt she couldn't go to Canada and leave him here.

"And after that?" Mrs Meade's concern was obvious.

Jane, touched, smiled at her. "I've taken a room with Mrs McDonald at the Post Office here."

Her employer smiled. "I suspect you don't really ever want to leave Ashburn."

"I do love it here," Jane admitted. "But I'm going to miss you all terribly."

It was late when she finally packed the last items into her suitcase. She looked round the room that had been hers for the last two years. The walls were pale green, the curtains framing the long window, brocade of a deeper hue. The bed had a luxurious downy, in soft colours, but the echo of green was everywhere. The furniture was solid, highly polished, giving the room a restful quality. It was the most beautiful room she'd ever lived in.

Jane curled up in the deep armchair and closed her eyes. She knew she'd never forget the peace and tranquillity of the Meade home, something very important to her. She wondered, savoured, what the future would hold. Would she ever find a family just like the Meades? She doubted it. Or a home, with a room as right as this one? But she refused to be downhearted. Surely she'd find something and who knows, it could be in a larger town, somewhere Kenny might enjoy living too. And after all, she'd be with children again and they were the most important thing.

★ ★ ★

Next day it was a somewhat forlorn figure who made her way to the single bus stop in Ashburn to wait for transport to Rowton. She'd never liked the town. Industrial, flat, a scarcity of trees, monotonous rows of identical houses, added up to the sum total of almost complete desolation in her view. She knew towns were necessary, that villages like Ashburn had to rely on them, but she was glad she had the choice of living where she pleased. Maybe at 24, people would think she was a bit young to be buried in the country, but she didn't agree.

By the time she reached the town, the early morning watery sun had been finally obscured by clouds and a persistent drizzle made her plastic mac cling to her tights and droplets of moisture were oozing into her shoes.

The street where Kenny lived just stopped short of being run-down. Last-ditch efforts had been made with paint on doors and windows but the brickwork on the houses was grimy and tired-looking.

Jane had met Kenny's landlady before and wasn't surprised to see she hadn't changed one bit. Mrs Brodie looked as expressionless as ever. A small woman, clad in serviceable clothes, of serviceable colours, the only startling thing about her was her hair. It was a delicate grey shade, waved softly about her ears.

"Yes?"

Although it came out as a question to Jane, the girl was sure Mrs Brodie knew at once exactly who she was.

"Hello, I'm Jane Ross. Kenny's sister," she smiled a little stiffly at the landlady.

"Come to tell me where he is then, have you?" the unwavering grey eyes stared at her.

"P . . . pardon?" Jane stammered. Mrs Brodie seemed to be asking the questions she wanted to ask. "You mean — Kenny's not here?"

"Not for three weeks now."

"What?"

"Not paid his rent, neither."

Jane felt fingers of panic clutching inside her. She'd never for a moment thought anything was seriously wrong. But he hadn't been here for three weeks! Where could he be? Surely he

9

wouldn't just go off without saying anything to anyone?

"Can I come in, Mrs Brodie?" she asked quietly.

Without answering, the woman held the door open wide enough for Jane to enter.

"May I go up to his room?" Jane tried to sound as calm as possible.

"I'll thank you to remove that dripping raincoat. Made enough mess in the hall here, no sense in trailing the wet upstairs too," Mrs Brodie closed the front door, none too gently, and indicated that Jane was to follow her up the narrow staircase.

There was an eerie quality to Kenny's room — as if he'd just walked out for a message and would be back shortly. His bed was neatly made but the rest of the room looked lived in. A blue shirt hung from the edge of the half-open wardrobe door, a pair of scuffed slippers lay on their sides under the chair. But it was the dressing table that drew Jane's eyes and tugged at memories. It looked

10

exactly like Kenny's old dressing table at their former home in Ashburn. It was cluttered, untidy, helter skelter.

With her index finger she gently poked among the assortment — sun glasses, clean handkerchief, nail file, book of matches, film programme, small change, paper clips, rubber bands, a folded magazine.

Jane half turned towards Mrs Brodie. "He'd hardly go off and leave all these bits and pieces if he wasn't coming back!" she said, panic subsiding in her at this very ordinary evidence of Kenny's day-to-day living.

"That's why I haven't re-let the room." Mrs Brodie's voice was as unemotional as ever, but Jane snatched at the faint hope that Mrs Brodie, too, didn't see anything sinister in his disappearance.

Her mind ranged over where he could be. Perhaps he'd gone to London to see a pop group. Sometimes these meetings went on for days. Maybe he'd got tangled with some girl. There were quite a few possibilities why Kenny hadn't returned. But why hadn't he let anyone know?

"I think I'll just check through Kenny's things, Mrs Brodie. I'm sure he won't mind," she smiled at the landlady but didn't move, making it obvious she wanted the room to herself.

Once she was alone, however, Jane was reluctant to start prying. Kenny might be her brother but his life was his own. On the other hand she could hardly just leave things as they were. Mrs Brodie was obviously anxious about her rent and the room might just hold a clue as to his whereabouts.

She opened the wardrobe door, automatically reaching for a coat hanger for the discarded blue shirt. She took out a dark suit — obviously Kenny's only one, and laid it on the bed. It didn't look as if it had been worn at all. She smiled to herself; Kenny hated anything formal. There was also a dark brown cord jacket and a blue anorak hanging in the wardrobe. A pair of training shoes sat on the floor.

It occurred to her that if she had a good assessment of the clothes Kenny had *left* in the room, she might be able to guess how long he would be away. She turned to the chest of drawers next, taking everything from the drawers and carefully laying the items on the bed, too. There was an assortment of shirts, jerseys, underwear and socks. Not much of anything and yet Kenny wouldn't have a lot of clothes; he didn't earn a fortune after all.

Jane paused. Kenny's job! Surely he hadn't left his job; he loved it, she knew that. Perhaps she should go along to his place of work and make some enquiries there, once she'd finished checking his clothes.

At the back of one of the drawers she found a bundle of the letters she'd written to him, what was obviously a Valentine card, though she didn't open it, and his bank book. Kenny had savings of £40. She held the slim blue book in her hand but she was puzzled. Surely if he had planned to travel far or stay away for a time he would have taken this? She searched again but there was no sign of her last letter to him.

Looking at all his belongings spread out before her, Jane instinctively knew that Kenny had walked out of this room expecting to return fairly soon — certainly well before three weeks. Cold fingers of fear were darting through her body. She turned again to the dressing table — there must be a clue somewhere in this room!

She picked up the magazine again and found three items inside — a postcard from Blackpool, a circular about a Sweepstake — and her letter! She turned it over. It was unopened. He must have got it before he left, so why didn't he open it? Maybe a letter from your older sister who was quite content to be buried in the country and who never had any exciting news anyway, wasn't worth reading. Of course, Mrs Brodie might have put this here after Kenny had gone. She'd go and ask her now.

Even as she turned she heard the door click. But it wasn't Mrs Brodie standing there. The doorway was filled by the tall, broad figure of a man. A man with a strong face; clean cut bones gave the head a good shape but the expression on the face was severe, angry and . . . Jane couldn't quite put a name to the other characteristic that marked the set of the face.

The man wore clean, but faded denims and a durable, ancient leather jacket. He hadn't moved from the doorway but she suddenly realised his expression and stance shouted aggression. There was something about this man that not only frightened her but put her on her guard. It was this last apprehension that made her hold her question, and fear, in check.

He spoke: "Thought you'd get away with everything, did you, Miss Ross?" The voice was as hard as the face.

Jane stared at him, then realised

that the pile of clothing on the bed must indeed look as if she was taking everything away.

"No, I was looking for — " she stopped suddenly. She had no need to explain to this person, whoever he was. "Who are you anyway?" she said.

By now he was leaning against the doorway, a sardonic smile on his face.

"I'm the man your brother robbed."

For a moment Jane swayed on her feet. His words hit her with the force of an explosion, but she recovered quickly to hit back.

"My brother isn't a thief!"

"He has my money, my week's takings. He has something which doesn't belong to him. I don't care what label you put on your brother, Miss Ross, but I want my money back — now! And you can tell him that from me."

"I don't know where he is!" she blurted out.

"Then why have you come to collect

his things?" The question was quick and sharp as an arrow.

"I haven't. I haven't heard from Kenny for a while and I came to Rowton to find out why."

"And you've discovered the bird has flown," he paused, lowering his voice but now the tone was even more menacing. "And now you know why."

Jane's heart was thudding unevenly. Kenny wasn't a thief. Not that! He'd never stolen in his life. There had been the usual orchard raids when he was a boy, and there was the time he and his pal had borrowed the doctor's sports car but they'd only taken it round the village of Ashburn.

Luckily, the doctor hadn't prosecuted and the police had let the boys off with a caution. High spirits, teenage wildness, mostly due to boredom in the small village, but never stealing.

She longed to sit down on the bed, her legs felt shaky, but she had no intention of appearing weak in front of this man. Besides, if Kenny had stolen

17

from this rude man, why weren't the police taking action?

Forcing herself to speak calmly she looked at the man in the doorway.

"Perhaps you'd better explain more fully just what business you have with my brother, Mr — ?"

This time the man's smile had all the characteristics of a sneer and she knew it was at her choice of words.

"Evans," he said. "Doug Evans, of Speedwell Services."

She nodded. Now she knew who he was — Kenny's employer.

"Kenny is one of my driver-mechanics," he continued, ignoring her nod. "Three weeks ago the week's takings were taken from the safe. Neither those nor Kenny have been seen since."

"And that makes Kenny guilty?"

"The combination of my safe, Miss Ross, is known only to myself and my clerkess — or rather my ex-clerkess," he paused significantly. "Your brother appeared to be interested in her."

Jane said nothing.

"Or he was using her," he finished quietly.

"Has she disappeared too?" Jane asked.

Doug Evans walked over to the chair and threw himself down on it.

"No, she's been dimissed."

"Why?"

"Because she gave your brother the combination of the safe."

Jane longed to sit down herself but sensed that any sign of weakness in her would be interpreted by Doug Evans as an admission of Kenny's guilt.

"Why?"

For a moment she thought there was a flicker of surprise in Evans's face, perhaps because she was being so persistent in knowing all the facts.

He spread his hands and began to explain. "I'd been away all week at the Motor Show in Birmingham. Cathie, my clerkess, had obviously been sickening for something, or so she says, and hadn't banked the takings each day as she was supposed to do.

According to her, she felt so groggy on the Friday morning that she had to go home. Kenny offered to bank the takings for her and so she gave him the combination of the safe." Doug Evans leant back, crossed his legs and stared hard at Jane.

"Bingo! No takings. No Kenny."

It was damning. Jane couldn't deny it . . . There seemed no other conclusion to come to but that Kenny had the money.

"You've checked that he didn't bank it," she said automatically.

He gave her a withering look.

"And this . . . Cathie?" she asked.

"Hasn't seen Kenny since she left the office to go home — or so she says."

Jane walked to the window and looked out on the unprepossessing street. Then slowly she turned round; she wanted to see Doug Evans's face when she asked her next question.

"And why, with all these facts, haven't you called in the police?"

Somehow she wasn't surprised when

he hesitated. She knew there was something not quite right about the whole thing.

"This was as much a disappointment to me as a shock," he was choosing his words with great deliberation. "Kenny's enthusiasm for his work and his skill, were really valued by me." The tone changed suddenly again. "That I should have been the victim . . . conned!" he drew breath again. "I want to hear from him. I want to know why he did it. I want to give him a chance to bring back the money he stole."

Jane looked at the hard, belligerent face of the man. He didn't look the type who would give anyone a second chance. From what she could gather, his clerkess had been summarily dismissed. Even had she not been convinced of Kenny's innocence, she would still have been suspicious of Doug Evans. The aggressive, closed face, the sudden accusations, obviously aimed at surprising information out of her, hid something.

Kenny's disappearance and Evans's accusations added up to a real nightmare, but Jane was more in possession of herself now. The first task was to find Kenny, the second to clear his name. She had no doubt in her mind that both his disappearance and the Speedwell Services money were linked. How, she did not know, but she'd find out.

"I'll find Kenny, Mr Evans," she told him.

"The super spy nanny on her bicycle," he said nastily.

"Did Kenny tell you about my job?" she asked, surprised.

"I do take an interest in all my employees," he replied. "Obviously not enough though." He paused. "I want you to find your brother. What I don't want is for you to walk out of that door so that I don't know where you are either."

"How did you know I was here, anyway?"

He laughed, but it wasn't particularly pleasant.

"Mrs Brodie telephoned me. She's an interested party too. You see, Kenny owes her money."

"I know that, Mr Evans," Jane snapped. "Don't worry, I'll stay in Rowton till I find Kenny."

"What about your job?"

"I don't have one now," she said, without thinking.

He immediately pounced on that. "Were you dismissed, or did you leave to get your share of my money?"

With great difficulty she held her temper in check.

"The family I worked for has gone to Canada. I . . . I didn't want to go."

Doug Evans studied her for a long moment.

"You haven't got another job?"

"Not yet," she said tightly. "But I have references and contacts."

He moved back to the door again and then turned to her.

"I'll give you a job. I've no-one in

the office since I sacked that silly kid, Cathie. You can work for me — "

"I don't want — "

"That way I can keep an eye on you. In fact, Miss Ross," he pointed a finger at her. "I'll pay you a good wage, if you work properly, but I'll keep a proportion of it as insurance. Insurance against the return of my week's takings."

"You've got a nerve to suggest such a thing. My brother is innocent, he didn't take that money!"

"Or I'll go to the police. Now. Today."

Jane stared at him. Would he go to the police? Should she call his bluff and refuse to take the job?

"Kenny's name and description will be in every police office in the country in a few hours' time, *if* I inform them," he said quietly, and she knew he'd read her thoughts.

No, she couldn't risk it, although she was fairly certain he didn't intend to go to the police. The last thing she wanted was to work for him and yet . . . surely Speedwell Services was the first place to begin looking for Kenny. If there were any clues to his disappearance they must be there. And if, as she suspected, Doug Evans wasn't being straight with her, what better way for *her* to keep an eye on *him* than in his own office?

"Well — " she began.

"Good. I knew you'd see it my way in the end," he smiled triumphantly.

"I can't type."

"You'll learn."

He was still smiling. "Have you a clean driving licence?"

"Of course," she looked at him defiantly. "I've never worked in an office before."

"It's a whole new adventure for you, Miss Ross. You can forget everything you ever learned as a nanny, you won't need that experience at Speedwell Services." He produced a business card from his pocket and handed it to her. "Be there tomorrow. 8.30 sharp." He turned and left the room.

Jane walked over to the door and closed it behind him. She flung the card on the dressing table and then walked over to the bed. She could at last sit down now that he was gone. Then the full realisation of everything she'd heard since he walked into this room swamped her and she collapsed on the bed, on top of all Kenny's clothes, uncaring, and wept.

But weeping wasn't going to help matters she realised after a few moments. She got up and went to the window. Outside the roofs were wet and slimy after the rain. A grey pall seemed to hang over the city. It couldn't have looked more uninviting or depressing. And she was stuck here until she found Kenny. And then what?

Oh, she'd managed to keep up a front of injured innocence before Doug Evans but she couldn't banish the fear that Kenny *might* have stolen the money. Perhaps those teenage escapades in Ashburn had been the beginnings of criminal tendencies. She bit her lip. Maybe she'd made a rotten job of bringing up Kenny.

They'd been on their own since their parents had been killed abroad six years ago, Kenny had been only fourteen then, at the most impressionable age possible. She'd known nothing about bringing up a teenager, but she'd tried, coping as best she could with all his difficult moods, helping him with school work, all the time she was doing her nursing training. Maybe she hadn't got through to him at all.

She'd worried for weeks over Kenny's request to leave Ashburn and find work in Rowton. He'd only been eighteen then and she'd thought he was so young to be alone in the city. But he'd never find a job in Ashburn — that had been obvious, and she herself had just secured the post with the Meades and they wanted her to live in. It had been the simplest thing to let Kenny go to Rowton, and give up the cottage which had been left to them by their parents. But it looked now as if she'd made the wrong decision. Alone in the city, without her guidance, he might have been desperate.

What if the temptation of all that money had been too much for him? What if he had been in debt? She opened his bank book again. Forty pounds. Was that all he'd managed to save since working here?

Desolation threatened to swamp her again. Deep down she was terribly hurt that Kenny hadn't contacted her over this trouble. Another fear clutched at her heart. What if he'd been unable to contact her? If he was hurt, or imprisoned somewhere?

She shook her head; her imagination was running riot, and speculation was only upsetting her more. She had to find him, had to begin somewhere. It was obvious that meant Rowton and now in Doug Evans's office. She shrank from that. It was the last thing she wanted, to work for that man, but she had no alternative. She had to get to know the people there, befriend them, get them talking.

She caught sight of her reflection in the mirror. She didn't look at all like Kenny. Her dark hair was in direct contrast to his blond head. She'd inherited her mother's hazel eyes, while Kenny's were blue. He was much taller . . . no one would take her for his sister and perhaps that was a good thing. She'd probably get on more easily at Speedwell if the other workers didn't know who she was.

Quickly and tidily she replaced all Kenny's clothes and personal belongings. Fears, panic, could be tamped down while she had a job to do, and she meant to get cracking right now.

She took her handbag, picked up Doug Evans's card and went downstairs. Although all the doors in the hall were closed, she was certain Mrs Brodie was listening behind one.

"Mrs Brodie, may I speak to you?" she called out clearly.

The landlady appeared almost at once.

Jane already had her wallet in her hand. "I'll settle Kenny's rent with you now. How much?"

Flatly, Mrs Brodie told her. Jane counted out the notes.

"If you have no other tenant for his room, I'd like to have it in the meantime. Same rates?"

Mrs Brodie stared at her then shrugged. "OK."

"Two weeks in advance," Jane said crisply, counting out more notes, thankful she'd saved well during her employment with the Meades.

"And I'm taking it in the name of Miss Jane Mitchell," she defied the landlady to argue.

Not a muscle twitched in Mrs Brodie's face. "Suit yourself. Evening meal, 6.30 p.m. If you're not here, it's not kept for you. Breakfast, 7.30 a.m. same rules." She pocketed the money and disappeared again into her kitchen.

Jane took some coins from her purse

and went to the pay telephone. She propped Evans's card against the wall and dialled his number. He answered immediately.

"I shall report for work tomorrow as you asked," she said slowly, giving him time to realise who was speaking, since she hadn't given a name. "I'm staying at Mrs Brodie's, and I wish to be known as Jane Mitchell."

There was a short silence from the other end of the line, then he spoke: "I have no objection to that."

"Thank you," said Jane with all the sarcasm she could muster and slammed down the phone. *He* had no objection! Did he think he owned her?

She picked up her suitcase and trudged up the narrow staircase again. Once inside Kenny's room she leant against the door and surveyed it with despondency. The walls were a monotonous beige, pale brown curtains framed the small window. A heavy duty cord carpet, of a colour that was either dark beige or muddy brown ran to within six inches of the walls. Highly polished linoleum surrounds made a sombre border round the dull square.

The furniture was cheap, light wood, with no character or exciting design. The bed looked clean but the bedspread was again as colourful as Mrs Brodie's dialogue.

A mental picture of her beautiful room at the Meades' home seemed to superimpose itself on this dingy room and she wondered for a moment if she would ever be able to live here for more than a day, let alone the two weeks she'd rented it for.

Wearily she put all Kenny's clothes to one side of the wardrobe and hung her clothes there, too. She allocated herself one drawer of the chest and unpacked her underclothes and personal belongings. She gathered all Kenny's bits and pieces and put them in a neat tidy pile at one end of the dressing table. They looked sad and incongruous with her toiletries arranged at the opposite end. The room seemed unable to take on any personality. It looked dull, depressing and threatened to defeat her.

Some time later Mrs Brodie knocked on the door and said she had some food for her. Jane couldn't have felt less like eating, but on the other hand she didn't feel like suffering the sharp edge of her landlady's tongue either.

To her surprise, the salad and sweet refreshed her and she had to acknowledge, although only to herself, that Mrs Brodie did know how to make coffee. There were no other lodgers at present, so she dined by herself.

Later that evening she donned her raincoat again and tramped round the streets of Rowton to look for 'Speedwell Services'. There were quite a few people out walking that evening. Jane was aware that she drew a few glances. She knew why. Here in Rowton the girls didn't dress in tweed skirts and heavy brogue shoes. Their clothes were smart, soft wool swinging skirts, high heeled shoes and pretty flowered blouses.

She found Evans's garage in Speed Street. It was an ugly squat building. Now it was shuttered and closed, the huge black doors bearing only the plain white lettering 'Speedwell Services'. The place looked clean and tidy, but somehow a little menacing by its very size; just like its owner, thought Jane.

Back in Kenny's room she looked through her own wardrobe of clothes. She must have something suitable to wear in an office, something the smart girls of Rowton wore. She wanted to look like one of them, wanted to fit in, so that no one at Speedwell Services would guess she was Kenny Ross's sister. But there was only one suitable outfit to wear — a flowery dress with a vee neck and cap sleeves. It was the smartest thing in her wardrobe. High heeled shoes and a white cardigan completed the outfit.

She had no idea what tomorrow would hold. The prospect of working in an office was daunting, but her worry over Kenny over-rode any personal reluctance. She went early to bed and tried to read a light novel, but it was no use, she couldn't concentrate and she didn't sleep too well either.

Breakfast at Mrs Brodie's was surprisingly good. Fresh orange juice, choice of cereal and bacon and egg. Normally Jane didn't eat much first thing in the morning and was on the point of refusing the full meal.

"You'd better eat this," the landlady said. "There's no fancy coffee breaks at Evans's place."

Jane obediently ate the lot, realising she would have few secrets from Mrs Brodie.

It was 8.15 a.m. when she arrived at Speed Street. This time the garage doors were open wide to the world. A few cars were parked on the forecourt and she noticed for the first time a small lean-to at one side of the building with the word 'Office' printed on one of the windows. She walked round to it but there didn't appear to be any door.

"What you lost, ducky?" a voice hailed her.

She turned round to find three men clad in dungarees watching her with some amusement.

"I'm trying to get into the office," she said primly.

"Want a car to hire?"

"No, I've come to see Mr Evans."

The men exchanged swift glances with each other.

"The office entrance is through the garage, m'dear," said one of the men, older than the others.

They stood back and watched her as she entered the garage. Inside it was like a deep, dark cavern. Several vehicles, cars, vans, pick-ups were ranged round the sides, some in various states of repair.

More men were working here, but they all downed tools to look at Jane. Whistles and calls followed her as she made for a small door at one side which she guessed led to the office. She grasped the handle, but it was locked.

"Good morning . . . Miss Mitchell,"
a voice boomed through the cavern.

She turned round. Doug Evans was
about ten feet away from her, his eyes
running over her outfit with faintly
hidden derision. The men had returned
to work, but she was aware that every
eye was on the two of them.

"Good morning, Mr Evans," She
steeled herself for one of his sarcastic
comments. She knew now she was
wearing entirely the wrong clothes. In
fact, slacks and sweater would be the
right things to wear here in this oily,
grimy place.

But he made no comment on her
clothes, just unlocked the office door
and ushered her in.

"Drop the 'Mr Evans'. Everyone
calls me Doug and that includes you."
He stood in front of her. He was
such a dominant person that as yet
she was totally unaware of the office
surroundings.

"Time means money to me," he told
her. "So I haven't got time to show you

37

more than one thing about running this office. You'll just have to pick it up as you go along. And I don't tolerate mistakes."

She faced up to him. "And the one thing?"

He stepped aside and she saw behind him a small, gleaming safe sitting on a squat table.

"I will show you the combination of my new safe," he said in slow, measured tones. "Then only you and I will have access to the money kept there." He moved forward and put one hand on the safe. "We shall just have to make sure that you don't yield to temptation, Jane, like your brother."

2

JANE shivered as she looked round the square, drab room where she was obliged to spend the rest of the day. 'Office' was too grand a title for this cubby-hole where the business of Speedwell Services was conducted. Decor was at an absolute minimum. If paint had ever adorned the walls it was totally obscured now. The wall to her left was covered with catalogues from manufacturers and suppliers of motor parts, tyres, oils, tools — all kinds of equipment — all totally incomprehensible to Jane.

Directly in front of her was a vast array of road maps, the centre one being of Rowton. It was liberally covered with red arrows and traffic alterations, such as new one-way streets, etc. Next to it was a bulletin board, showing telephone numbers of hospitals, hotels, airlines, ferries. Appropriate flight and sailing times were also shown.

A small scarred and battered desk stood at right angles to the wall on her right. This wall held a square window which overlooked the forecourt. On closer inspection Jane noticed there was a sliding glass partition and that the inside window ledge was as wide as a good shelf. No doubt money changed hands here, thus affording the office a little security. An old-fashioned, high-backed dining chair, with stained rexine seat had been pushed against the desk. Jane pulled it out and gingerly sat down.

Now she was face to face with an ugly black monster of a typewriter. She didn't need to be told it was ancient. It had an unusually long carriage and a multitude of keys, letters and figures, all dusty and uneven. Even to her inexperienced eye, the typewriter looked temperamental and unreliable.

A grey filing cabinet was against the opposite wall, alongside the gleaming new safe. Box files cluttered up another corner and a well-used trolley supported a dented kettle, half a packet of tea and a sad looking packet of biscuits.

Jane felt her spirits sink to their very lowest. What on earth had she taken on? She had no alternative though; she had to be here to find out what had happened to Kenny and why. The quicker the better, too. As soon as she found her brother she'd be shot of this place!

She rummaged in the desk, found some paper and took out her pen. Now she was ready for anything. As if on cue, the telephone rang. She found the instrument behind the typewriter on the narrow desk.

"Hello," she said hesitantly into the mouthpiece. "Er . . . Speedwell Services."

"Manson here," the voice said. "Put me through to Doug please."

Put him through? Jane stared at the telephone for a moment then noticed there was a small board by the instrument with two switches, numbered 'One' and 'Two'. Her fingers hovered over the switches. How on earth did this thing work?

"Hold on, please," she said as brightly as she could. She laid down the receiver on the desk and ran out into the garage working area.

"Mr . . . er, Doug. Phone call for you."

"Put it through on Two," the deep voice called from the depths of the workshop.

Her heart sank, she'd been hoping he'd take the call in the office. She returned to the telephone, lifted it and looked at the tiny switchboard. Presuming it worked on the same principle as light switches she put the 'Two' switch down, and listened for the connection. There was a sharp click and she heard the dialling tone. She'd cut him off.

She went out into the work area again. "I think I cut him off by mistake," she called out.

"I think you have," Doug mimicked her voice. "Get him back on the phone and pronto. He's our best customer."

When she got back into the office, the older mechanic she'd noticed on arrival was waiting there.

"I'll show you, love. Get Manson on the phone, there will be an address book in the desk somewhere."

Jane looked at the man with gratitude. He was in his middle fifties, she guessed. Hair was sparse, eyes were a little faded, and his colour was poor, but there was a friendly smile on his round face.

"The boss is a bit rough, but you'll get used to him."

"Will I?" Jane sounded unconvinced, but she found Manson's number and dialled it quickly.

"Now," the mechanic leant over the small switchboard. "When he comes through, ask him to hold on and flick Switch No 2 up. The phone will ring in the far end of the garage and Doug will answer it. Tell him

Manson is there and put the switch on the down position. They can talk then. You'll hear a buzz when they're finished and you put the switch back on the level."

After making apologies to Mr Manson, she did exactly as she'd been told and the call went through smoothly.

"Thanks," she smiled up at the man.

"Tom's the name," he grinned and leant against the trolley.

"I won't forget what to do, Tom. I daren't," she laughed.

He looked at her frankly. "How come you took this job? It doesn't seem your style, somehow. You should be in one of those fancy offices, up town."

Jane shrugged. "I was made redundant. Lucky to get this job, really. All seems a bit strange first day."

The switchboard buzzed and she put the No 2 switch level.

"What did you do before you came here?" Tom asked.

Jane paused. She couldn't say Nanny. It was possible that Kenny had told someone in the garage about her.

"I worked for a businessman, in the country." That wasn't a lie, she just didn't say what her job had been. "Got to get used to a big town now," she smiled at Tom. "Plenty of maps here to help me."

"You got somewhere to live?" Tom asked casually.

She hesitated again. If she said Mrs Brodie's, it could still connect her with Kenny. She had to be vague about it.

"Not settled yet. Got a room at the moment, but I expect to move on."

She hadn't heard the office door open, but suddenly Doug was standing beside Tom and she knew he'd heard her words. She knew, too, what conclusion he would draw from them.

But he wasn't looking at her. "Finished for the day then, Tom?"

"Just came in to see if them sparking plugs had arrived, Doug." Tom slid out of the office like an eel, without another look at Jane.

"And have they?" Doug turned to her.

"What?"

"The sparking plugs."

"I . . . I don't know — "

"There's no time for gossiping here," Doug told her.

"He showed me how to use the switchboard," she said in defence of Tom.

"Humph. And I'll show you the mail, since you haven't even bothered to open it yet." He lifted a pile of letters from behind the typewriter and shook them before her face. "I need to know what's in these first thing every morning. I can't afford to lose customers — by phone or letter!" He pointed at the window. "There's a customer wanting attention."

Jane jumped up and slid the window open. A businessman stood there, account and chequebook in his hand. She took the account from him, remembering she'd seen a receipt stamp on the desk. She found it, receipted the account and exchanged it for the cheque. The man thanked her and walked away.

She looked at Doug. "I'll put this in the safe," she said, pleased that she hadn't stumbled over the transaction.

"You saw that he put his address on the back of the cheque, or his bank card number?" he asked lazily.

Even before she turned the cheque over, she knew the back would be blank.

"Let's hope it doesn't bounce — for your sake," Doug said. "I'll bank the takings today and explain at the same time that my new clerkess will be doing it in future," he left the office.

Her mouth set, Jane put the cheque in the new safe. Doug was being unfair. Any girl would be at sixes and sevens the first morning in a new office. But she'd never worked in an office before and he knew that. He wasn't making it easy for her. He was a hard man.

But she could be determined too. She began to search through the desk, to familiarise herself with whatever she could find. One drawer held a pile of books, each clearly labelled and inside was a record of appropriate business. She laid them out on the desk: 'Car Hires'; 'Accounts'; 'Postage'; 'Orders'; 'Repairs'. Briefly she glanced through each one and noted the format. They were all well organised and clearly laid out. She could detect different styles of writing. Obviously Doug had had a succession of clerkesses. Not surprising, if he treated them all so brusquely.

The morning sped past. She didn't have much time to study the books as customers came to the window, rang up with queries about their cars; and several repairs had to be booked in.

One phone call was quite terse. "Imperial Hotel here. Car for Councillor Carpenter in fifteen minutes please."

She told Doug and was amazed when he looked into the office a few minutes later, resplendent in grey suit with matched peaked cap.

"I'll be out for a couple of hours. I have to do this job myself as I'm a driver short." He paused significantly and she knew he was referring to Kenny. "Keep all messages for me."

As soon as he left the premises, Jane felt herself relax. A little of the tension was gone and she realised she was hungry. She was amazed to find it was twelve-thirty. He had said nothing about a lunch break and she wondered if she was expected to work on, or if she should lock up the office and go and find a cafe or lunch bar.

It soon became apparent that everyone relaxed with the boss out of the way, as one by one the other mechanics began to drift in and out of the office with petty questions and vague enquiries. She soon began to realise that she was being given the 'once-over'. She didn't mind, it was only natural and she was pleased to find that Doug's staff on the whole seemed a nice crowd. It would take her some time to memorise all the names, but she took particular note of Angus and Bert, both lads in their late teens who might just have been friends with Kenny.

"We're going round to the chippie to buy something to eat, can we bring you something, Jane?" Angus asked her.

The last thing she felt like was anything fried, but it would obviously be tactless to refuse on her first day here. She had to get on with everyone.

"That would be great, I was wondering what I could get to eat."

"The last girl, Cathie, used to bring sandwiches," Angus said.

"That was because she could have her lunch in the park with you-know-who," Bert grinned.

Angus laughed and winked. Jane felt her pulse quicken. They must be referring to Kenny. Doug had told her he was sweet on Cathie. She said nothing, however. It was much too soon to start asking questions. The boys left her and Tom came in to enjoy a cigarette and, she suspected, a break from work.

"What do your Mum and Dad think of this job, then?" he said casually.

"Oh, my parents died in — " she stopped. She simply had to be more careful. Even the smallest item could link her with Kenny. " — some years ago," she finished.

"Any brothers or sisters?"

"All on my own," she smiled falsely at him, a little chilled by the fact that she could lie so easily.

Well, perhaps it hadn't been an actual lie, just an evasion of the truth, as when she'd said she'd worked for a businessman. For a moment she debated whether to confide in Tom. He'd been so kind and she did need an ally. But just then the telephone rang.

"This is Miss Dalrymple here," a slightly tremulous voice said. "And I'd like to speak to Kenny, please."

Jane's mouth dried up completely.

"Oh . . . well, I'm not sure . . . "

"Now, now, I know it's not permitted for Kenny to come to the phone, but

I also know that Mr Doug is away for lunch, so he won't know anything about it. You did hear me say it was Miss Dalrymple, didn't you?" The voice had taken on a peremptory tone.

"Yes, I did, but — " What on earth could she say to the old lady? How could she explain Kenny's disappearance? Then she realised that Tom was still in the office, and watching her, and that she was not supposed to know anything at all about Kenny.

She put her hand over the mouthpiece. "Did I meet all the chaps here this morning? This lady is asking for someone called Kenny and I don't remember — "

"He ain't here."

"Is he off sick?" Jane asked innocently.

"Dunno. Boss tells me nothing," Tom said, his chubby face absolutely expressionless.

"I'm so sorry, Miss Dalrymple," Jane spoke to the old lady again. "But Kenny isn't here. Can I get someone else for you?"

There was a short silence from the other end of the phone.

"No, you can't get anyone else for me. You know I only like being driven by Kenny. He's always so kind, so thoughtful. It's no picnic having to go to hospital for physiotherapy and the journey would be impossible without Kenny. What am I to do?"

"I can only offer you another driver," Jane said. Obviously this was a regular trip that Kenny made with the old lady. "When is your appointment?"

"Tomorrow. And I don't want anyone else. Just Kenny." The phone was very firmly replaced at the other end of the line.

"Oh dear, that's quite a problem," Jane said. "I'll have to ask Doug when this Kenny is due back. Is he a young chap?"

"Yeah. He's a mechanic, but he also drives the taxi cars when Doug needs him." There was a twist to Tom's mouth as he said this, and Jane wondered if there had been some trouble over Kenny's dual role.

Just then Angus and Bert arrived with chips and sausage rolls and Tom left. Jane thoroughly enjoyed her lunch and over a cup of tea, settled down to study the various record books in the desk. The latest entries had all been recorded in a round girlish hand and after a while it dawned on Jane that this must be Cathie's work. If she should need anything explained she could always contact her. Her address was probably in the office's address book. Just to check, Jane leafed through it, wondering about Cathie's surname. She found an entry — Cathie Johnson, Cakewalk Crescent — in the same round hand that had made the entries in the business books.

As she was putting a slip of paper in to mark the page, an idea struck her — one she should have had ages ago, she realised. She could contact Cathie anyway! She might know something about Kenny, something that she'd been too scared to tell Doug. Jane decided to phone her right away since Doug was out of the way and the men were still at lunch.

She dialled the number, her heart beating with excitement and anticipation. The phone rang and rang and rang. Eventually, she had to give in to the fact that there was no reply. But she did have Cathie's address and there were plenty of maps on the wall to tell her how to get there. She checked at once. It was not too far from Mrs Brodie's. Jane made a quick copy of the map in the back of her diary.
She'd visit Cathie tonight. The decision made her feel a lot better.

When Doug returned she gave him a note of the messages for him, then mentioned about Miss Dalrymple's phone call.

"She was insistent that Kenny should call for her and she didn't give me a chance to say who would come in his place. Which of your other drivers would do?"

Doug leaned against the trolley.

"None, really. She's a fussy old bird and only Kenny knows how to handle her."

"Would you go yourself?"

"Ha!" he gave a short laugh. "She can't stand me."

"It's nice to know that someone thinks well of Kenny," Jane said with a touch of asperity.

Doug's expression changed immediately. "She doesn't know what he's done, does she?"

"What he's alleged to have done," Jane's answer was even swifter than his.

He left the office immediately.

She rolled some paper into the typewriter and began a stabbing attack with two fingers on the uneven keys. But her thoughts were not on her typing. It hadn't occurred to her that the customers would know Kenny, too. She must try to find out as much as she could about him from them, too. But it would have to be done subtly. She could hardly ask each one if they would give a character reference for Kenny.

Doug came back into her office just before five o'clock.

"I've decided," he said abruptly. "You can take Miss Dalrymple."

"Me? But I'm your clerkess. I don't — "

"You're employed by me," he emphasised. "I tell you what jobs you do. And you said you had a clean driving licence. But I'm not a hard man," he grinned sardonically. "I won't throw you in at the deep end. Miss Dalrymple likes to be driven in comfort. She goes in our white wedding Cortina. You can take it home with you tonight. Drive it around, locate her street."

"But tomorrow — what about the office?"

"I'll look after it. You won't be away long. Just a short trip. Don't think I mean to make a habit of this. I don't intend you to become one of my drivers — gives you too much leash. But this time I don't want to lose a valuable customer."

Jane banged away noisily at the typewriter as Doug left the office. The man was impossible!

* * *

She reflected that it must have taken a tremendous effort on Mrs Brodie's part not to comment when her new lodger arrived home from her first day at work in the firm's wedding car. But Jane might as well have come home on roller-skates for all the notice Mrs Brodie paid.

It had taken Jane a little while to get used to the car and she was glad she had the opportunity of a little preparatory drive. After her meal, she set off for Miss Dalrymple's home in Newberry Terrace. She found it without much difficulty and then took the route from there to Speedwell Services and back again. No problems, except for one wrong turn she took on the way back. She was surprised that there was a faint familiarity about the street name — Cakewalk Road. Then it hit her. Cathie Johnson's address was Cakewalk Crescent. It must be around here somewhere. She could just pop in now and save a walk later.

She found No 16 Cakewalk Crescent just around the corner. There was no reply to her knock. She kept it up for as long as possible. Maybe Cathie was still unwell and in bed. But eventually she drew the attention of a neighbour.

A thin woman appeared at the door next to Cathie's.

"Nobody in. Who you wanting, anyway?"

"Miss Johnson."

"She's away."

"Oh — on holiday?" Jane asked.

The woman stared at her. "You a friend of Cathie's? Don't reckon I've seen you before."

Jane thought fast. "I'm the new girl from Speedwell Services. Just wanted to ask her something about . . . er . . . the invoices."

"Oh. Well, she'll be back in a day or two."

Jane had to be satisfied with that. The woman was going to give nothing away. And questions about invoices hardly sounded life and death problems. She wondered if she should have told her the truth. That she wanted to know about Kenny. But then again, only two people in this whole town knew who she really was — Doug and Mrs Brodie, and she wanted to keep it that way.

She looked round Cakewalk Crescent. A short road, modest houses, a few cars, but no one else about. At least — her heart almost stopped as a man stepped from a blue mini. It was Doug.

He walked across to her, his tread slow and menacing. She stood by the door of the white car trying to steady her shaking legs. He lightly kicked the Cortina's rear tyre.

"This is not a Jane Mitchell run-around, you know."

"I only did as you instructed — found

60

the route to and from Miss Dalrymple's house."

"With a little detour to Cathie Johnson's."

Jane looked at him defiantly. "I intended walking round to Cathie's tonight. When I took the wrong turning and found myself so near I thought I might as well call on her."

"Took the wrong turning deliberately."

"I didn't," she flared. "You forget I don't know this town."

"Wasted your time, anyway. No-one there. Where is she?"

"The neighbour didn't say," Jane muttered, then realised what he'd said. "Have you been following me?"

He nodded.

"That's despicable, don't you trust — " She stopped.

"No, I don't. I gave you the car for two reasons. The first I told you in the office. The other? I thought you might just lead me to Kenny."

"I don't know where he is!" she almost shouted at him, yet mindful that they were still in Cakewalk Crescent and Cathie's neighbour might be listening.

She opened the door of the Cortina. "There's no need to follow me now. I'm going straight back to Mrs Brodie's. And I'll pay for the petrol tonight," she got in and slammed the door.

He leant down and looked through the window.

"Of course. I'll deduct it from your wages," he said.

* * *

Jane had calmed down by the time she returned to Mrs Brodie's. In fact, she was trying to think rationally. There was something most odd about Doug's attitude. It was as if he was trying to rile her all the time. Yet surely if he thought she knew anything about Kenny, his best plan would be to be helpful. That way she might be lulled into trusting him. But she'd never do that now. There was something sinister about his whole attitude. He claimed Kenny was guilty and yet he hadn't reported him to the police.

Anyway, that was her first day at Speedwell Services over. She hadn't achieved much in her search for Kenny but perhaps tomorrow would be better. Remembering Doug's outfit when he took out the hired car, she selected her grey pleated skirt from the wardrobe. She didn't have a matching jacket but her navy blue blazer looked smart enough. A white blouse completed the ensemble. Remembering also the dusty state of the office she decided to take along the flowered smock she'd worn when playing messy games with the Meade children. That all seemed years ago now, she reflected ruefully.

She detected a fleeting look of surprise and approval in Doug's eyes when she drew up in the car the following morning. She parked it carefully and went into the office. First thing, she opened the mail, attending to some of the accounts which had been paid, and arranged the letters in what she considered to be some order of importance. Doug came in and took up his usual stance leaning against the old tea trolley. He quickly read through the letters then looked up at Jane.

"Right — do you think you can acknowledge this lot? Just log them in the appropriate record book, I'll show you where — "

"I know. I went over them yesterday. I think I'll manage those."

"Good for you," he smiled very slightly. "We don't post receipts. The customers can call and collect them — up until one month after payment. After that destroy them." He caught her eye. "If, of course, you are still here at the end of the month."

She said nothing and worked hard until it was time to leave to fetch Miss Dalrymple. Doug came back into the office and settled his large frame as best he could at the small desk.

"I know how long it used to take

Kenny on this run. I'll expect you back here in ninety minutes," he grinned slyly. "I hope you can think up some convincing story to tell her about Kenny's absence."

Jane parked directly outside Miss Dalrymple's house. It was an old stone-built town house, with a wide flight of about a dozen stone steps. She pressed the bell and heard it peal loudly inside the house. The front door was in keeping with the age of the house — a frosted glass panel, surrounded by a well-kept wooden frame. A lace curtain hung primly behind the glass.

After a few moments the door was slowly opened and Miss Dalrymple stood there. Small, stooped slightly over a stick, she had a bright alert face with eyes which very quickly assessed Jane from top to toe.

Miss Dalrymple's mouth trembled slightly. "Wouldn't Kenny come for me?"

"He's away at the moment — something only he could do, Miss Dalrymple,"

Jane said hesitantly.

Fortunately Miss Dalrymple took her statement at its pure face value.

She nodded knowingly. "I understand. I know he's the most valuable man that Speedwell Services has so naturally he has all the important jobs to do. Do you know, my dear, I think Kenny will eventually take over that business. He's clever and competent and has such nice manners. Not like the dreadful owner."

Jane silently agreed with her opinion of Doug but she only said: "Oh really? By the way, I'm Jane."

Miss Dalrymple disappeared into the hall, calling over her shoulder. "Perhaps you'd help me with my coat then, Jane. Kenny always does."

With her trained nurse's eyes, Jane had realised that Miss Dalrymple was an arthritis sufferer. Obviously one hip was badly affected but her hands and elbow joints were swollen too. With practised hands she assisted the old lady into her coat.

"Kenny locks the door for me too," she handed Jane a key.

As she began to help her down the stone steps, Miss Dalrymple said crossly: "No, no, don't hold my arm like that! Oh dear, I suppose you're doing your best, but no one is quite like Kenny. He knows exactly what to do. His sister is a nurse and I expect he's learned it all from her." Miss Dalrymple moved Jane's hand a fraction down her arm. "There — that's just right."

Jane held her tongue. After all, she more than Kenny knew exactly how to handle patients, but this was a moment for tact. She settled the old lady in the car and started the engine.

"Makes such a difference when one is properly trained," Miss Dalrymple began talking as soon as she was comfortable. "Nursing is such a caring profession. You look an intelligent girl — whatever made you take on working for Speedwell Services? With a little training you might have become a nurse yourself. You should ask Kenny how to go about it."

Jane hid a smile. Obviously the old lady liked to talk, so maybe it could be put to good use.

"I've only begun working at Speedwell, Miss Dalrymple, and I haven't seen this . . . Kenny . . . there, yet. I take it he's a nice type."

"The very best, my dear. I would trust him with my life."

"Would you consider him honest as well then?" Jane asked casually.

"But of course! You mustn't tell that man Evans, but Kenny does odd little jobs about the house for me, in his spare time of course. I have lots of valuable ornaments and silver plate in my house, and with me being so slow on my feet, thieves could be in and out before I'd notice. Kenny could have slipped anything away, but I know he wouldn't. I trust him implicitly."

Once again Jane was tempted to reveal her true identity, but caution held her back. Miss Dalrymple was a chatterbox and might unwittingly give her away to someone at Speedwell Services.

She returned to the Speedwell garage almost exactly ninety minutes later. Tom was hovering about the forecourt.

"Where shall I park this?" she called, as several more cars were ranged around the forecourt.

"I'll put it away, Jane. Boss always likes it cleaned and polished after every run and we can't expect you to do that. Where have you been? Out with Kenny's old dear?"

"I've been with Miss Dalrymple," she said quietly, but she was happy inside. According to the old lady, Kenny was a pure 22-carat gold character. And obviously, if he'd been a thief, he would have taken the opportunities offered in her house. "I'm afraid I was a poor substitute for him. He's some kind of wonder boy according to Miss Dalrymple," she told Tom.

He looked at her closely, the chubby face again set. "Aye well, there's some good actors around, with two faces, you know what I mean?" His voice was loud and a little strident.

His remark was like a cold douche to Jane and what was more she saw Doug standing only a few yards away, the knowing look on his face confirming he'd heard every word of her conversation with Tom.

As she went into the office it occurred to her that Tom had wanted Doug to hear the conversation. She wondered why. Perhaps Tom was jealous of Kenny's abilities and the popularity he obviously enjoyed with Miss Dalrymple. It struck her then that none of the men had mentioned the missing cash in connection with Kenny. Didn't they know about it?

She flung her bag on the desk and looked at the pile of letters waiting for replies. With uncertain fingers, she arranged letterheads and copy paper with carbons and began the task of typing. She wasted paper after paper as she couldn't get the hang of typing at all — even with two fingers. One of the boys brought her a salad roll at lunch while she slogged on at the letters. Hours seemed to pass and she was getting nowhere. Doug came in from time to time, just giving her and the crumpled paper sardonic looks, but making no comment.

Then she produced a reasonably typed letter only to find she'd put the carbon in the wrong way round. She put her head down on the old black typewriter. It was no use, she couldn't continue with this job. She hated it. The sight of the clean and gleaming hospital where she'd taken Miss Dalrymple that morning had made her feel very nostalgic. The familiar crisp white uniforms, the air of efficiency and healing, the orderliness . . . how she longed to be back nursing. Maybe she could say to Doug that she'd take a job at the hospital and pay him back from her earnings there. It wouldn't be so easy to look for Kenny then, but she wasn't getting anywere here. She couldn't stick it, she'd —

The telephone rang. As she lifted it, she heard the familiar bleeps of a pay-call phone. With a sigh she got her pad and pen ready to take a message.

A voice spoke urgently before she could say more than: "Speedwell Services" —

"Cathie, it's me. Don't speak, say nothing, I expect Doug's hanging around as usual. I don't want him to know it's me. I'm in a real jam. Not much money. I'll phone you at your house tonight. Seven o'clock. For God's sake be there, Cathie love." The pips began. "I've no more money — "

The phone went dead on Kenny's voice.

3

"KENNY, Kenny!" Jane said desperately into the telephone mouthpiece, knowing it was no use, knowing her brother had hung up the telephone. Slowly her hand replaced the receiver but her brain was racing, trying to play back in her head every word that Kenny had said.

Of course, he hadn't known he was speaking to her. The line was bad and when he heard her answer he'd obviously assumed it was Cathie Johnson.

But his message had been pretty clear. Certain of his words were burning in her head — 'Not much money' surely must mean that he didn't have the garage takings. It seemed a small light in the darkness of those desperate words. 'Real jam' sounded pretty bad — and not at all innocent.

She would know nothing more until she spoke to him tonight at seven. She would have to be at the Johnsons' house then when he rang.

It struck her then that since Kenny didn't know Cathie had been sacked, that he had not been in touch all this time. She'd better phone Cathie immediately.

She lifted the telephone and dialled the Johnsons' number. It wasn't until it rang several times that she remembered Cathie was not at home.

Panic began to take over. If Kenny got no reply when he rang tonight, they might lose touch again. He was in trouble and needed help, there was no doubting that. He needed someone to talk to. Besides, she wanted to know where he was as soon as possible, to try to sort this thing out.

She had to find Cathie, get her home by tonight. She'd go back to Cakewalk Crescent and somehow get the girl's address from the taciturn neighbour.

Meanwhile she had to carry on in

the office until five-thirty as if nothing had happened. She still had a pile of letters to re-type. This time she'd get them neat and correct, She did, but the hands of the clock were creeping near to six o'clock when she'd finished. Valuable time would be lost if she went to Mrs Brodie's for tea. Tonight she'd better skip the meal and make straight for Cathie's house.

"I can't afford to pay you overtime."

She looked up to find Doug standing by the office door. He moved towards the desk and she handed him the letters to sign.

"I wouldn't dream of claiming it. It was my own inexperience and inability that caused the delay."

Doug laid the letters on the desk beside the typewriter and bent over to sign them. Suddenly he looked up and stared at her. His face was only about eighteen inches away from hers.

"I didn't expect you to stay late to finish them. Tomorrow would have done. I'm not completely inhuman, you know. I know you've never typed before and that this machine is a devil to handle." His eyes no longer held the slightly derisory, mocking gleam that she'd come to expect. "It was a joke about the overtime," he tapped the letters. "And you've made a good job of these, untrained or not."

"It took me long enough," she acknowledged dryly, leaving the desk and hanging her smock on the peg.

"I'll run you home."

"Oh no!" Jane whirled round to face him. She didn't want to go home, but he mustn't know that. She slipped on her jacket and tried to look casual.

"I wouldn't dream of putting you to all that trouble. I need some fresh air, anyway."

"It's no trouble. In fact, I insist!"

"I'd rather you didn't — "

"Look, Jane, there are no strings attached, I'm not following you around tonight. You're pale and tired. Today's been a strain, so come on!"

His perceptiveness and unexpected

kindness threw her a little off balance and she was lost for a reply. As a result, she had no alternative but to get into the car, otherwise he would have become suspicious and she certainly didn't want him playing watch-dog again.

She raced through her meal at her lodgings, feverishly trying to think of a reason for rushing out again. She wouldn't put it past her landlady to phone Doug if she was suspicious about Jane, too. After all, she'd done it before. And then she remembered the letters. Having come home all the way by car, she'd forgotten to post them.

"I'll skip coffee tonight, Mrs Brodie," Jane said as she rose from the table. "I forgot to post the office mail."

"Better look sharp. Last collection is at seven from the box on the main road," Mrs Brodie nodded at the clock on the sideboard.

Jane hurried all the way to Cakewalk Crescent, pausing only to shoot the letters into the pillar box as she passed. She hammered on the door next to the Johnsons' house. The woman opened it, looking even more annoyed than the evening before.

"Sorry to bother you, but I must contact Cathie. Something happened in the office today which I must speak to her about." Jane's voice was firm but polite, and the authority in it got over to the woman.

She hesitated only briefly. "She's at her aunt's. Ross Avenue, number ten. Two streets away, that direction." She pointed out the way to Jane.

"Thank you, you've been most helpful," Jane smiled.

She tried not to run, she didn't want to be noticed, but it was ten to seven. The door of number ten Ross Avenue, was opened by a slim, fair girl. There was a certain winsomeness about her small heart-shaped face that instinctively told Jane this was Kenny's girl. She was just the type to appeal to her brother.

"Cathie . . . hello. I'm Jane Ross, Kenny's sister. Look, I can't explain anything now, we haven't time. Kenny's phoning you at your house at seven o'clock. Can we go there now?" It was an abrupt and dramatic way of introducing herself to Cathie, but there was no time for preliminaries.

For a second or so, Cathie stared at Jane, her blue eyes startled and worried.

"K . . . Kenny?" then she seemed to pull herself together. "My key — " she turned from the door. "It's upstairs, shan't be a moment," she called over her shoulder to Jane as she ran for the stairs.

Jane waited in an agony of impatience on the doorstep, even though the girl took only half a minute.

"I'll scribble a note to my aunt, she's out at the moment and she's expecting me to be in all evening!" Cathie grabbed a small pad by the telephone and began writing furiously.

Then they were out of the house and

began to half-run, half-walk along the pavement.

"You know where Kenny is?" Cathie asked.

"No, I don't, but he phoned the office today and said he'd phone tonight. He thought he was speaking to you," Jane told her.

"The office?" Cathie was totally confused.

"Please, Cathie, trust me, just come to your home and wait for Kenny's call. I don't even know where he's phoning from. We must hurry."

"I thought you were a nurse," Cathie said as they rounded the corner of Ross Avenue.

"I am — well, was," Jane said. "My job sort of folded. I came here to see Kenny and found he'd gone."

"This is a short-cut." Cathie pulled her arm and they ran down a narrow lane between the houses, which Jane hadn't noticed earlier.

"You know why he's gone?" Cathie asked breathlessly as they crossed the

Crescent to her house.

"I know about the missing takings," Jane answered grimly.

They raced up the steps of Cathie's house and the girl opened the door . . . to silence. Jane looked at Cathie and then her eyes followed the girl's gaze. The clock on the wall said seven-ten.

"Oh no!" gasped Jane and looked at her watch. There was no mistake. After all that rush, they were ten minutes late!

"We've missed him," Cathie's voice was near breaking point.

"He'll try your number again," Jane said with a conviction she didn't feel. There had been something so specific about phoning *at seven*. If the time hadn't mattered, Kenny would just have said 'tonight'.

"What if he doesn't?" Cathie persisted.

"Can we sit down somewhere," Jane dodged the question.

Once in the living room, Jane briefly told Cathie the story of her arrival in

Rowton and why she was now working at Speedwell Services.

"That awful Doug is making you work with him? He really scares me, Jane. I'd never have stayed in that job if Kenny hadn't been there." Cathie reached in her pocket for a handkerchief. "That man was so horrible when he came round to see me after Kenny had gone."

"Cathie, I really want to know what happened that day the money went missing."

"Kenny didn't take it," the girl said at once.

"No, I don't think he took it either, but — "

"Think? I know he didn't take it, Jane."

Jane took a fresh look at Kenny's girlfriend. She might appear soft and a little weak, but there was no doubt of her loyalty towards Kenny.

"If he'd wanted to take money, he could have done so at any time. He'd watched me open the safe often enough.

He said it was too much responsibility for me to have, and he was my security guard." The girl smiled a little tremulously at the memory. "And he always drove me to the bank."

"But not on the day he went missing," Jane said.

Cathie shook her head. "I was ill that day and Kenny insisted on running me home. I didn't want to go as Doug was away and I was supposed to bank the takings for him. Kenny said he'd do that and bring the receipt round to me in the evening. We'd keep quiet about it. He left me and went back to the garage to get the money . . . And I haven't seen him since," she whispered.

"When did you find out that the money had gone?"

"Doug came round to the house that night. Someone had reported to him that neither Kenny or I had been around that afternoon. Doug noticed the takings had gone and so he came to me for the receipt." Cathie stopped for a moment. "Of course, I had to tell him that I didn't have it and that Kenny had promised to bank the takings. I can't tell you what he said when he discovered I'd told Kenny about the safe. He was awful, shouting and accusing me . . . I told him to ask Kenny. He said Kenny had better come up with the goods." Cathie's voice failed her.

"What did he mean?"

"The bank . . . had phoned him in the afternoon and asked why Speedwell Services hadn't made their usual deposit." Cathie paused and then went on in an even quieter voice. "He went storming round to Kenny's digs and discovered he hadn't been there all day."

"Kenny wasn't planning to go away, all his clothes are still there," Jane said.

"I know," Cathie sobbed. "I had no idea what had happened to him. It's been awful these last three weeks, Jane."

Jane went over to the girl and put an arm round her. It had been much worse for Cathie than it had for her.

"I thought the most awful things — that he'd been mugged or abducted, left lying somewhere to die," her voice faded. "Well, he isn't dead, but we still don't know where he is or what happened to him."

They had been talking fairly quietly in case even the slightest sound drowned the ring of the telephone, but the silence from the hall hurt their ears.

"Why doesn't he ring, Jane? Where is he?"

Jane shook her head helplessly. She had no answers for Cathie. The girl was now anxiously twisting a gold necklet with her fingers. Cathie caught Jane's eye and she unclasped the necklet and held it out to her.

"Isn't it beautiful? Kenny gave it to me."

Carefully Jane took the necklet in her hands. It was beautiful. Real gold in a twisted rope design. It was also very, very expensive.

"I have a bracelet to match." Shyly

Cathie showed Jane the gold rope bracelet.

"I can tell that Kenny is very fond of you," Jane said conventionally, but she was trying to hide first her surprise, then anxiety about the obvious value of the gifts. She didn't doubt her brother's affection for the girl, but how could a garage mechanic afford to buy jewellery like this on his wages? It wasn't as if Kenny saved money; she remembered those meagre forty pounds in his bankbook.

"Do you mind about me?" Cathie asked anxiously, obviously a little upset by Jane's worried expression.

"No, no, I'm delighted," Jane said sincerely. "I'm really happy that Kenny has such a nice girl."

Whatever Kenny had done, this girl had not led him into it, Jane was sure of that. She was too open and honest. There were no artifices about Cathie Johnson.

Suddenly Cathie seemed to divine Jane's worry.

"Kenny used to make some extra money working in his spare time."

"For Miss Dalrymple," Jane smiled.

"Oh, you know!"

"I met Miss Dalrymple and she told me about him," Jane nodded, but in her heart she knew that the money Miss Dalrymple paid Kenny would not have bought those expensive gifts.

"She's been ever so good to him," Cathie told her.

Jane said nothing. She was remembering the glimpse she'd had of Miss Dalrymple's house — beautiful old furniture and unusual ornaments, but the curtains and carpets had been worn and shabby. Miss Dalrymple had some fine heirlooms in her house but she didn't have the money to replace worn furnishings. No, Miss Dalrymple could not afford to give Kenny much in the way of payment.

The girls talked for a little while longer but their minds were not on the conversation. The telephone did not ring.

"It must only have been convenient for Kenny to ring at seven," Jane said eventually. "It's almost nine-thirty now, I don't think he'll phone tonight. I'd better go home and I expect you want to go back to your aunt's. I'll walk round with you."

"Kenny will think I've let him down." Cathie was distraught.

"I'm sure he knows you too well for that. I expect he'll phone the office tomorrow," Jane said comfortingly, wishing she felt as confident as her words.

"I'm coming back home tomorrow," Cathie said firmly. "I've only been staying with my aunt because my parents are on holiday and I was ill. And . . . and I didn't want Doug to know where I was."

"That's why your neighbour wouldn't tell me where you were the first time I called," Jane said.

Cathie blushed. "I'd told her not to tell anyone where I was . . . except Kenny, of course. I was scared Doug might come back, but I don't care now. I'll be back here tomorrow in case Kenny phones."

They walked together to her aunt's house and Cathie asked her to call again the following evening.

Jane was worn out when she reached her lodgings. Her brain was too tired to conjecture any more about Kenny that night. He was alive; that was the important thing. She slept deeply but awoke feeling tired and drained. A few letters arrived just as she was leaving the house, but she only had time to stuff them into her bag, unread, before rushing to the garage.

Doug and she were going over the mail just after eight-thirty when the office phone rang. Being nearer to it, he lifted it and as he did so, Jane distinctly heard the pips of a pay-phone. What if it was Kenny?

"Speedwell Services," Doug said clearly, and the pips stopped at once.

"Huh. Somebody not used to a pay-phone. They'll ring again." He put the receiver down and returned to studying the mail.

Jane slid her hands under the desk so that he wouldn't see them trembling. It must have been Kenny, hanging up immediately he heard Doug's voice. She forced herself to calm down and listen to Doug's instructions about the mail. One thing was sure, Kenny wouldn't ring back right away since he knew Doug was in the office.

"We'll go to the bank today," Doug was saying. "I'll show you the routine for paying in the takings." He looked at his watch. "Be ready in half an hour. Better start counting the money now. Lock yourself in the office while you do it. I try not to take any chances," he finished on a note of slight sarcasm.

Jane did as she was told and opened the safe. Although she'd been depositing cheques and cash from paid accounts since she'd begun working with Doug, she hadn't actually totted up the grand total. She was amazed at the final figure — and she'd only been here three days. When Kenny had disappeared a whole week's taking had gone, too. How much had that been? And where was it now?

She waited outside on the forecourt for Doug, the money-bag clutched in her hands. She listened to him giving instructions to the men, his manner tough and aggressive.

"Right, Tom. I want that Vauxhall ready for the road when I come back. We can't keep the customer waiting any longer, even though you may not be worried. Angus! Have you stripped the van brakes yet? What are you waiting for, Christmas?"

The men nodded at him and immediately got back to work. He was a hard taskmaster thought Jane, wondering why Kenny had stuck it so long here.

Doug showed her into his Mini. "Lock the door and fasten your seat belt," he said brusquely.

He settled himself in the driving seat and looked her over to see that everything was in order.

"I've got it all safe here," she patted the money-bag.

"Quite a tidy sum, is it?"

"Yes, I was surprised," she told him.

He gave her a shrewd sideways glance and smiled tightly.

"I though you might be." He swung the Mini out of the forecourt and onto the main road. "I reckon the takings from the car hire is the biggest proportion. You see, most of my customers need regular transport, so when their own cars are in for repair I rent out another one to them. It's good business, but I have to be absolutely fair and have their own cars repaired as soon as possible. Otherwise it would be dishonest."

She said nothing, but knew he was quietly explaining why he kept his men so busy. She had to admit he was in the right, too.

"How did you begin — with repairs or hired cars?"

"Repairs. I worked on a financial knife-edge at first. Eventually I got a car of my own but had to hire it out, and travelled around Rowton on my bicycle," he laughed. "It was the only way. I started too early and finished too late for public transport."

"The self-made man," Jane commented.

"That's it, and I'm not ashamed of it, nor particularly proud for that matter."

"There's nothing to be ashamed of," she said reasonably. "And it is an achievement."

He drew up at traffic lights and turned to look at her. He seemed to weigh up what she'd said and then he shrugged, but she had seen a small smile at the back of his eyes.

At the bank he introduced her to the teller who dealt with the firm's business. The transaction was simple and she knew she would have no difficulties with it in future.

"I intend to drive you here each time, but if anything unforeseen should occur and I'm not available, you are not to come here on your own; do you understand, Jane?"

"I won't run off with your money, Doug," she said wearily, getting back into the Mini. "That wouldn't solve anything."

"I know that." He slid into the driving seat, but didn't start up the engine. "I was thinking of your protection, believe it or not." He looked at her very directly.

"Sorry," she mumbled. "I'll remember."

"Have you heard from Kenny?"

"I haven't been able to contact him," she said stiffly, choosing her words.

"Jane, I want to help you. I'd like to find Kenny too, and not only to recover my money. I don't like what's happened, I don't understand why he should just disappear like this."

She looked at him. Once again he seemed concerned and the hard look was gone from his eyes and jaw.

"I was pretty rough on you the day we met, but I was anxious about

Kenny and I didn't think you had much knowledge of town life, and Rowton is a hard town, believe me. I've taken knocks, many knocks, and I may run a successful business now but there are some in this town who'd like to see me fall flat on my face."

Jane hesitated. She was very tempted to tell him about Kenny's phone calls. It wasn't in her nature to be secretive about anything, and she knew she could do with some help. Cathie was a sweet girl, but she wasn't much good in a crisis, Jane had realised that last night. She longed to discuss the whole matter with someone mature, someone who might have a less emotional point of view.

"Anybody who does me a bad turn, mind you, lives to regret it." Doug was staring over the driving wheel and out of the windscreen.

She caught her breath. How could he say one minute that he wanted to help find Kenny and spell out revenge in the next? Yes, Rowton was a hard town, and Doug was one of the hardest men in it. The fact that he hadn't reported the missing money to the police was still a mystery to her. Telling Doug anything might mean more trouble than ever for Kenny.

"I'll remember that," she said quietly.

He whipped round to face her. "I don't take revenge on kids, even if they have done me a bad turn, which I don't think is the case with Kenny."

She turned away to look out of the car window, but said nothing. After a moment, Doug started up the car and drove back to the garage in silence.

She worked steadily until lunchtime when Angus looked in and offered to bring her some salad rolls from the delicatessen along the road.

"Yes, please," she smiled and then sat back to relax for a bit. Looking in her bag for money to pay Angus, she found the letters she'd grabbed so hastily as she was leaving her digs that morning.

Fortunately, she'd given all her

friends Kenny's address and she was touched to find there was a postcard from the Meades sent before they boarded the aircraft for Canada. There was also a letter from Miss McDonald, the postmistress at Ashburn village where Jane had lived all her life. There was a third envelope, too. The address was typed on the front; Jane opened it, somewhat mystified. Inside was a small business card. It was engraved with the name 'Pretty Puma'. That was all. Nothing else. No address, no telephone number. She turned it over. The other side was completely blank.

"Here we are, Jane, salad sandwiches and yogurt. Must be how you keep that smashing figure." Angus came in with his mate, Bert, and they unpacked Jane's lunch.

She laughed at the remark. They were nice boys and she took no offence as none had been intended. They chattered to her for a moment and then, just as they were leaving, she remembered the card.

"Hey, can you tell me what Pretty Puma is? A boutique, cafe? Disco?"

"Where did a nice girl like you get to hear about the Pretty Puma?" Angus asked.

She hesitated. For some reason she was reluctant to say the card had been sent to her.

"Found this card in the mail." She didn't specify whose mail.

"It's a gambling club, Jane. A real smart joint, for those who have big money."

"And some who haven't," Bert murmured.

Jane looked at him enquiringly.

"That card is probably meant for Kenny Ross. You know, the guy who used to work here. Miss Dalrymple was looking for him the other day."

"I remember," Jane said faintly. "But . . . but why should a garage mechanic need a card for this place?"

The boys exchanged swift glances.

"He used to go round there some evenings. Mad, crazy, he was we used

98

to tell him. Gambling's a mug's game . . . Nobody else in the garage knows about this, so get rid of that card fast, Jane."

"But surely a garage mechanic wouldn't have money to gamble?"

Angus shrugged. "Not on our wages he wouldn't, but I think Kenny mostly went there for kicks. Don't get us wrong, Jane, Kenny Ross is a nice guy, me and Bert both like him; and when he fell for Cathie Johnson we reckoned it was the best thing that could have happened to him. Cathie's a real sweet kid."

Jane had to bite her tongue as she had been about to answer 'I know'. She couldn't let on that she'd met Cathie — not yet.

"Funny that Kenny should stay away so long," Bert said. "I really hope nothing bad has happened to him."

"Don't tell me we're talking about the boss's blue-eyed boy again," came a sarcastic voice from the doorway.

They all turned to find Tom, the

slightly seedy man, watching them sardonically.

"He was a good worker, Tom, he didn't swing the lead, or eavesdrop." Angus pushed past the mechanic and left the office, followed by Bert.

"Good riddance to bad rubbish, that's what I say about Ross," Tom said to Jane.

"Before my time, so it's none of my business," she said firmly.

She didn't encourage Tom to talk any more and soon he left too. Left her with her thoughts, which were disturbing to say the least. Kenny, a gambler? But surely he couldn't have afforded that? And surely Cathie would have known? But the expensive jewellery . . . the missing takings . . . had they paid off a gambling debt?

Jane dismissed the thought. That was just being ridiculous. These things only happened to big-time gamblers. Angus's theory that Kenny went to the club for kicks sounded much more likely.

There was no doubt that Angus and Bert really liked her brother, that they didn't think of him as bad. But Tom . . . his dislike of Kenny was really quite patent. She wondered why he was so vindictive towards her brother. Surely not only from jealousy because Doug had given Kenny the best jobs? After all, Tom was old, hadn't much of an appearance and must be fairly near to retiring.

Jane ate her lunch without really tasting anything. She looked up at the clock, willing it to move to five-thirty as swiftly as possible. There had been no further pay-phone calls all day, so she guessed Kenny was leaving it until the evening. She decided to ring Cathie and check if she had moved back into her own house. Doug was still out somewhere so it was fairly safe. Cathie answered immediately and Jane brought her up to date with the news that Kenny had phoned earlier.

"So, he's still all right, Cathie, don't worry on that score. He just didn't want to talk to Doug."

She didn't hear Cathie's reply as someone knocked at the counter window on the outside wall. Reaching over, she slid it open slightly.

"I'm speaking on the telephone, can you wait a moment, please?" she only caught a glimpse of a man outside.

He popped his head round the window and said: "Actually I'd like to come into the office, if I may. I want a word with Kenny Ross." His voice was pleasant and slightly deferential.

Jane could only see his face, but he looked friendly. It was impossible to tell if he was a garage mechanic or not as she couldn't see what he was wearing, but he might be a friend of Kenny's. Someone she could talk to, even confide in!

"Yes, please come round to the office would you?" She tried to hide her eagerness.

"OK. Be right with you," His face disappeared from the window.

She picked up the telephone again.

"Cathie, someone has called about Kenny. Must go, tell you about it later tonight. Bye for now."

With her hopes high again, Jane tidied her desk and quickly ran a comb through her hair. There was a brief knock at the door and then the visitor entered. He was fairly tall, slimly built, with thick fair hair which he was trying to settle with his hand. His face was open and friendly, blue eyes smiled hesitantly at her.

"Good afternoon. Can you tell me where to find Kenny Ross? I have some business with him."

She hardly heard his words. Now she could see what he was wearing. Police uniform.

4

THE policeman was smiling tentatively at her. Her mouth moved a little, but it could scarcely be called a smile. Her facial muscles seemed frozen.

"Do you know him?" he asked as Jane remained silent.

"Yes," she managed to get her paralysed tongue round the word. Then panic gripped her. "No!"

The policeman wasn't smiling at all now, just looking at her with a polite, questioning expression on his face.

"S-sorry, bit mixed up. I'm new here," she said jerkily.

With mounting apprehension she saw him take a notebook and biro from his pocket.

"This . . . this Kenny Ross hasn't been around since I started work here, but I've heard of him. Everyone's been talking about him," the words came out in a rush.

"Oh really?"

The two words seemed so innocent yet Jane sensed a quick alertness behind the casual question.

He stared at her for a moment. "How new are you, Miss — ?"

"Mitchell. Jane Mitchell. I've been here about two weeks."

He nodded. "Two weeks. I see. And you haven't seen Ross. So, he hasn't been at work for a couple of weeks?"

She didn't reply.

"Does he often do this — disappear for a couple of weeks?"

"I . . . I don't know," she shrugged.

"Not to worry, I'll ask some of his mates in the garage." He made to leave the office.

"No, don't do that!" Jane blurted out. She had no idea what Doug had told the men about Kenny's absence but she didn't want them knowing about her brother before it was necessary.

The constable turned slowly on his heel to look at her.

"Why not?"

"They don't know anything, either. I mean, nobody knows where he is."

"Nobody?"

Jane tried to calm down. She was making an absolute mess of this. The constable was looking at her in a most suspicious manner.

"I mean, I don't think he told them where he was going."

"Who's in charge here?" He looked around.

"Doug — Mr Evans. He's out at the moment."

"I'll wait. Perhaps he can tell me something about this Kenny Ross."

Jane stifled a gasp. That was the last thing she wanted.

"He may be ages. Perhaps I can help you?" she asked, her heart in her mouth, terrified of what she was about to hear. Maybe she could keep this quiet for a little longer. Just enough time for Kenny to come back to Rowton of his own free will and not be brought by the law.

"Yes, perhaps you could," the constable said slowly. "You have his home address here?" He leant on the table and opened his notebook.

"Er . . . " Jane hesitated. She was reluctant to give him Mrs Brodie's address. If he found out she was living in Kenny's room, it would look most odd.

"Well . . . I'm not sure," she delayed.

"It must be on the files."

"Yes . . . yes, it must, but I shall have to ask Doug first. He's ever so particular."

"Miss Mitchell, have you ever heard of Greenhill Youth Club?" the constable asked.

"Youth club?" she repeated vaguely. What on earth was he on about now?

"Kenny Ross coaches the Youth Club football team. But the boys say he hasn't been around lately."

Jane felt a ring of ice round her heart. Kenny's absence was beginning to be noticed by others outside the garage.

She thought desperately. "Oh well, perhaps he's away on holiday." Anything to stop this search for Kenny. "Perhaps he's visiting relatives." She thought that was inspired.

"We understand he has a sister. Maybe we'd better check on her."

Oh no! Then the trail would lead right back to Rowton and this office!

"Do you think that's really necessary?" she asked.

"Don't you think it's rather odd that a young lad should disappear like this, Miss Mitchell? If he was your brother for instance, wouldn't you be worried sick?"

Jane fought to conceal her feelings, to hide her expression.

"You don't really know if he has disappeared, do you?" she said slowly. "Has . . . has someone reported him missing? I mean," she gathered all her courage together. "I mean, why are the police looking for him?" She sat tense, waiting to hear the worst.

To her amazement the constable laughed.

"The police aren't looking for him. Just me! I want to help him with the football team. The boys told me he worked here and asked me to find out when he was coming back."

"Oh, I see," Jane's voice was faint with relief. Kenny was safe! Safe for the time being.

"So, it's all quite simple, isn't it?" he said very directly. "Nothing sinister, is there?" He was smiling but it was obvious from his tone that he thought she had put an entirely sinister complexion on a trivial matter.

Jane smiled briefly at him, wondering how on earth she could possibly explain away her attitude. Unless she could, the police would become curious about Kenny and that could lead to disaster.

While excuses and explanations were chasing around in her head, the office door swung open and Doug entered. With a swift, unsmiling glance he took in Jane's strained face and the presence of the policeman.

"Well, constable, what's this?" he said brusquely. "What business have you here?"

The constable hesitated for a fraction and Jane could see a deferential attitude being quickly replaced by a brisk official one.

"I'm Constable Nelson. I came about Kenny Ross."

Dough abruptly sat down on the edge of Jane's desk, obscuring her view of the constable.

"What about him?"

"I only wanted to speak to him." The constable's voice held no warmth now.

"He's away," Doug said shortly.

"So I've gathered from Miss Mitchell. When do you expect him back, sir?"

"Depends on how long it takes." Doug swivelled round and picked up the mail, as if the constable was dismissed.

"How long what takes?" the policeman persisted.

Doug gave him a cursory glance.

"The training scheme. Heavy goods vehicles, transporters — that kind of thing. He won't be back until he can handle everything like an expert. I don't hold with second-best in Speedwell Services, constable."

"I see." The surprise and puzzlement in the policeman's voice was obvious.

"What is it about, anyway?" Doug asked.

"The local football team haven't seen this Ross for a few weeks."

"Well, they wouldn't, would they, if he's away?"

"That's quite true, Mr Evans. My apologies for wasting your time." His voice was icily polite. "Goodbye, Miss Mitchell." He left the office.

Doug sat on the desk for a few seconds, his back to her, then got up quickly. "I could use some coffee."

Jane rose stiffly from her chair and walked over to the small table where the kettle sat. Her body was still tense with apprehension. She turned round to find Doug watching her.

"Thought for a moment he'd come to give us bad news," he said.

"Bad news?" she was puzzled.

"That something had happened to Kenny. Accident. Found injured — that kind of thing."

She wondered if that was why Doug had sat on her desk, shielding her from Constable Nelson.

"I didn't think of that. Thanks, anyway, for saying about the training scheme — that was a great idea," she smiled at him.

But he wasn't smiling back. "You didn't think . . . it didn't occur to you that he might have been the bearer of bad news. Why did you look so upset then?" He caught her arm and turned her round to face him. "Are you trying to tell me that you thought he'd come about the money?"

Jane wasn't a good enough actress to hide the truth of her feelings. He slammed his fist on her desk.

"I told you I haven't spoken to the

police about this." He was livid. "When will you believe me? I'm trying to give your brother a chance. If you can't trust me, we're going to get nowhere," he said with emphasis.

"I'm sorry . . . I panicked. It was the only thing I could think of," she said.

He lowered himself into the small rexine-covered chair in the corner, his eyes never leaving her face.

"If the fact that the police wanted to question Kenny was the only thing you could think of, then you weren't worried that he'd had an accident or anything," he spoke slowly, thinking out the situation.

Jane sat tense.

"Therefore you know he's all right."

She said nothing.

"You've heard from Kenny." It wasn't a question.

Still she kept silent.

"You might have told me!" he blazed.

"I — I haven't spoken to him. I don't know where he is. I just know he's alive," she told him, unable to meet his gaze.

"I see. Who did he telephone, Cathie Johnson?"

She nodded. "But, please don't go and see her. She's afraid — "

"I know. I scare her silly. It's my quick temper. Some people can take it. Some can't." He leant forward in his chair. "You'd better get this straight, Jane. Keep me informed about Kenny. Tell me everything you know about him. But only me. There's no way that brother of yours is going to get out of this mess without my help. Got that? If you don't do as I say, you — " he stabbed a finger at her " — will be in trouble up to your neck, too." He got to his feet. "Keep the coffee, I couldn't force it down." He slammed out of the office.

Jane sat looking at the two steaming mugs of coffee, feeling absolutely shattered. She'd been so glad to see Doug and when he'd told the policeman about the fictitious training

114

scheme, her heart had soared with relief and gratitude towards him. He *was* protecting Kenny and did believe in him. For one wild crazy moment she'd thought she might tell Doug everything about Kenny, enlist his help. But now — now he was as bullying as ever. He wanted to get Kenny back — on his terms. Was he taking the law into his own hands?

So how could she trust him? He'd told her he was a self-made man and that anyone who did him a bad turn lived to regret it. Why then was he just accepting the fact that one of his drivers had apparently run off with over a thousand pounds? Could he afford to be without that cash? Jane knew he couldn't. Surely there must be some alternative motive behind his acceptance. But what?

Did he know more about the missing money than he'd let on? Was he really in Birmingham on that day? Jane had heard of people staging robberies in their own offices in order to claim insurance. Had Doug put Kenny up to this kind of job and somehow it had all gone wrong? Perhaps Kenny had realised how wrong it was and that was why he'd run off. If so, then Doug was a dangerous character indeed. But of course she'd no proof of this . . . not until she'd spoken to Kenny, anyway.

She'd have to be careful now not to make Doug too suspicious about Kenny, make it appear as if she was keeping him in the picture about her brother. She worked hard for the rest of the day, her only comfort being in the fact that once again she had another aspect of Kenny's character.

From what Constable Nelson and Doug had been saying, it was obvious that her brother was involved in voluntary community work. If he did that why did he go along to the Pretty Puma gambling club? She picked up her handbag and took out the Pretty Puma card. Why on earth would it have been sent to her?

Jane was weary when she arrived back at her lodgings that evening but once again there was an appetising meal awaiting her. Mrs Brodie was plain and unadorned as pease pudding, but her cooking was fantastic.

"Minestrone soup OK?" She put a bowl in front of Jane.

Jane felt her troubles slide from her shoulders as the aromatic steam rose from the bowl.

"Parmesan cheese?" Mrs Brodie's worn hand passed the dish.

As Jane sprinkled the cheese over the soup, Mrs Brodie pulled out a chair and sat opposite her, something she never did.

"Italian meal tonight, hope you like it," she said in her flat, unemotional voice.

"I love continental food." Jane hid her surprise at her landlady's attitude.

"H'm," Mrs Brodie grunted. "I hear you deserve it. Working hard at the garage. Doug says you're a good worker, like your brother. He liked fancy food, too. There's lasagne next. Fresh peach for dessert. No wine, don't hold with drink."

Jane hid a smile. Mrs Brodie would go so far, but definitely no further. But there was a faint glimmer of contact here, too. Obviously Doug had been chatting to her. And Mrs Brodie hadn't mentioned Kenny since the day Jane had arrived.

"You must have got to know Kenny fairly well?" she asked casually.

"So-so."

"I heard he runs the youth football team."

"Dirty boots and socks all over the place."

"I admire him, giving up his spare time like that," Jane said stoutly.

"Aye, some of his spare time."

"Did you like his girlfriend?" Jane asked, wondering at the same time if Mrs Brodie knew Kenny spent some spare time at the Pretty Puma.

"Cathie Johnson's a nice kid, I know her folks well. But Kenny's too young to get married," the landlady replied quickly.

"But you think he's good enough for her?"

She didn't fool Mrs Brodie. The grey eyes faced her across the table.

"I said he wasn't ready for marriage. I didn't say he wasn't fit for it."

Jane smiled. It was a grudging character reference, but it was obvious Mrs Brodie just thought Kenny a bit young and perhaps irresponsible. If she'd thought him bad, she'd have told the Johnson parents without hesitation.

Mrs Brodie knew nothing about the Pretty Puma. Jane was sure of that. Because she knew that someone of Mrs Brodie's type would not 'hold with gambling' any more than she would with drink, and Kenny would have been thrown out of her house if she'd had any suspicions.

★ ★ ★

119

As soon as Cathie opened the door to her later that evening, Jane knew she'd heard from Kenny. Her face was alight with happiness.

She grasped Jane's hands and pulled her into the house.

"He's phoned! He's phoned! And he's fine, Jane. He's all right. Isn't that wonderful?"

"Yes, yes. Now tell me everything," Jane said anxiously.

Cathie sat opposite her on the sofa, her eyes sparkling.

"Well — he said he'd phoned the office this morning but Doug answered — "

"Yes — "

"So he thought I must be off ill again and phoned here. Oh, I'm so glad he did. Just to hear his voice again, Jane, it was wonderful — "

"Yes, of course," Jane bit on her impatience.

"Anyway, he's fine, okay — "

"Where is he?"

"Oh, well, he didn't actually say — "

"Did you ask him?" Jane was frantic.

"Well, you see, the pips kept going and he had to keep putting money in. But he's fine, Jane, he's got a job."

"A job? But his job is here, at Speedwell!"

"Yes, but this is until he comes back."

"But when is he coming back?"

"Oh, soon, he didn't actually say when."

Jane almost despaired. "Cathie, the money. What did he say about the money?"

"He said nobody would believe him about that — about what happened."

"But he can't just stay away for ever. Has he got the money?"

Cathie was beginning to wilt under the barrage of Jane's questions. Her eyes looked anxious, then moist.

"I don't know, Jane. I — I didn't ask him. I was just glad to hear his voice, and that he still loved me — "

Jane dropped her head. Yes, maybe that was important, more important to

Cathie than getting this mess cleared up. She wouldn't know, she'd never been in love.

"I just wish I knew where he was and when he was coming back."

"Oh, he did say," Cathie thought hard. "Yes — he said he'd be back when he was ready to clear up everything."

Jane stared at the girl, trying to analyse that statement.

"When he was ready to clear up everything" — there was only one answer to that. Kenny *was* involved with the missing money. Jane could have cried. She so much had hoped that somehow he was innocent, totally innocent. She had to hide this from Cathie, though. She realised the girl was in too emotional a state to be told that Kenny was a thief and would have to face justice when he returned.

When he returned? Jane began to wonder if it would be 'If he returned'.

"I managed to tell him that you were working at Speedwell Services, Jane."

Cathie suddenly remembered. "He'll phone you there."

"Didn't he wonder why I was there?"

"No, he didn't have time to ask. I told you, Jane, the pips kept going. He just said: 'She's what? Tell her I'll phone.' The whole conversation was like that. Just quick bits of talk."

Jane realised it was no use asking Cathie any more questions. She'd obviously been too excited to think straight when speaking to Kenny and beyond knowing he was all right and that he loved her, she hadn't questioned any more.

She told her about Constable Nelson's visit, but said nothing about the scene later with Doug.

"The police still don't know Kenny's missing." Cathie was jubilant. "Oh, everything's going to be fine; you'll see, Jane."

Jane had coffee with Cathie and then left. Unhappy and distressed she walked around Rowton for a long time thinking about her brother. Kenny was obviously somewhere far away. The recurring pips on the phone indicated he was making a trunk call. He had a job, therefore he was earning money. For what reason? To replace the takings? But surely he couldn't have spent over a thousand pounds? That was frightening. And then she remembered about the gambling club. She knew Angus and Bert, the two mechanics from the garage had not been lying when they told her Kenny went to the club from time to time.

Looking around, she realised she was in the town square. It was a cold, concrete place, the wind pushing papers into corners, the flowers in the tubs looking petrified under the street lamps. Plenty of people about, yet the loneliest place in the world. Her eye alighted on a phone booth and she knew what she was going to do.

Inside the booth she flicked over the telephone directory pages and found the address of the Pretty Puma. Outside again, she stopped the nearest couple and asked directions.

She realised as she took the route that she was entering an older part of Rowton. The buildings were rundown, almost derelict, with broken windows and graffiti on every available wall. The pavements were festooned with litter and children ran about in the dark, dodging pedestrians and cars alike. Eventually, the houses petered out and the road was bounded on either side by waste ground, peppered with old prams and cardboard boxes and the odd stripped-down car. Ahead, Jane could make out a square building, isolated amid the rubbish dumps, its garish neon strip lighting giving an enticing impression of colour and warmth.

She approached the building warily. 'Pretty Puma' was spelled out across the face of it and a vague caricature of a big cat was outlined in neon. The place had once been an uninspiring two-storey house. Now, all the windows were covered with wire, giving an impregnable appearance to the club.

Only the sound of pounding music escaped out to the street.

Several cars were parked outside but the front of the club was dominated by a huge American car, shining black, its wings and preposterous fins outlined in chrome. It was a flashy vehicle and seemed to shout the word 'gambler' at her.

There was nothing beyond the club, just a black, derelict night. With panic, Jane realised that she had no alternative but to enter the place. To turn round and go back the way she'd come would look highly suspicious to the half dozen or so loiterers watching her.

With a bravado she certainly wasn't feeling, Jane pushed open the club door. Inside she found the garish lighting was continued. Electric blue walls and fitted carpet shouted at the emerald green cloakroom counter. Bright orange lights gave a nightmare quality to the interior. Behind the counter a vividly made-up woman ran her eyes over Jane with practised assessment. "Yes?" she asked, above the noise of the fruit machines rattling away in the hall.

Jane realised that she looked totally out of place. No one would ever think she'd come here to gamble. She would never get away with that.

"I'm . . . looking for a job," she blurted out.

The painted eyebrows were lifted dramatically. "As what?"

"Office worker."

"Here?" the woman laughed derisively.

"You must need someone to keep the books in order," Jane said daringly.

The woman lifted the counter flap and swayed past Jane.

"Wait here. I'll see if the boss has a minute to spare," she said with heavy sarcasm.

A few moments later she reappeared from the end of the corridor.

"Second door on the left," she pointed sulkily.

The door opened as Jane approached.

A man stood there, big, heavily built, running to fat. His face proclaimed his profession had once been in the boxing ring, but only his eyes were still alert. He didn't speak. A voice came from behind him.

"Do come in, young lady."

Jane's heart was thumping erratically. Whatever happened now, she must keep her cool; it was the only way she could find out about Kenny's visits to this club.

She stepped into a dark, panelled room, with plain brown carpet and heavy oak furniture, a startling contrast to the garishness of the entrance hall. The man behind the desk facing her was a surprise, too. He didn't stand, but she could tell he was smaller than average. He had neat grey hair, curling slightly above the ears and mild-looking eyes behind gold-rimmed spectacles. His suit was a clerical grey and he wore a spotless white shirt and sober silk tie. He reminded her of her family doctor at Ashburn.

"I understand you're looking for a job, Miss — " he said.

"Mitchell. Jane Mitchell," she said in as firm a voice as she could muster. "I'm new to Rowton and a little hard up. Thought you might have some evening work. I mean keeping accounts," she finished hurriedly.

"That's your line, keeping accounts?" he asked, with mild curiosity.

"I'm experienced with ledger work."

"M'm." His eyes had never left her face and Jane realised that there was something behind the mild expression, something she couldn't detect.

"My accountant will be here on Thursday evening. I'll ask if he needs some help. And I'll telephone you, Miss Mitchell. May I have your address and telephone number, please?"

"Oh . . . er, well, I'm not quite fixed permanently yet. Perhaps I could call again?" She couldn't possibly give them Mrs Brodie's address, they might connect her with Kenny. Besides, whether she got a job or not she now had an excuse to come back.

Amusement flickered briefly in the man's eyes.

"You do that, Miss Mitchell."

"Thank you, Mr — " Jane said, realising the interview was at an end.

"Reyburn. Carl Reyburn."

A moment later, Jane was back in the corridor, her legs a little shaky. Carl Reyburn couldn't possibly know about her, yet there had been something off-key about that brief interview. She didn't like this place one little bit and her impulsiveness might be something she'd regret later. Still, if she got the job she might have a chance of finding out if Kenny was in trouble with the smooth Mr Reyburn.

She opened the front door and stepped outside into the night. The darkness momentarily stunned her after the fluorescence of the club. She made to hurry in the direction of town but bumped into someone standing outside. The man held on to her.

"Just a minute, ducky, no need to

hurry. I could do with some company tonight."

"Let me go!" Jane struggled to shake off the man's grip, but he began to pull her towards the club again.

They had almost reached the door when she heard a car sweep into the kerbside and stop abruptly. The grip on her arm loosened immediately and the man slipped into the club.

Jane turned to look at the car. It was a police Panda and the neon club lights illuminated the driver as he came across to her. There was no mistaking that tall, slim figure and the thick fair hair. It was the policeman who'd been in her office that morning. Constable Nelson.

"Hello, whatever are you doing here? Lost, are you?"

Jane nodded quickly. "Yes, on my way home now." She could hardly tell him she'd just applied for a job at this place.

"I'll take you. This is no place for a lady." He helped her into the car. "I guess you're new to Rowton as well as Speedwell Services," he said as they drove off.

"That's right. And thanks for turning up at the right moment, Constable Nelson."

"Alan," he said, giving her a warm smile.

"It was silly of me to walk around here alone," she said, but didn't give a reason.

"I wouldn't have thought a girl like you would have to walk around alone — anywhere."

She accepted the compliment with a smile, but said nothing.

"Jane, I'm off-duty in twenty minutes. Would you like to wait for me and we'll grab a cup of coffee before I take you home?"

"Yes, I'd like that."

Twenty minutes later she was sitting in Alan's rather draughty and tired Morris. He drove her to a small cosy cafe.

"How long have you been in Rowton,

Jane?" he asked as soon as they were settled in a booth.

"Just a couple of weeks."

"Where are you from?"

She didn't want to say Ashburn, because that might connect her with Kenny. Some of the boys at the youth club might know where Kenny had been brought up.

"From the country — can't you tell? Who else but a bumpkin would go wandering around like I did tonight?" She hoped she'd divert him from finding out exactly where she'd lived before.

"Was it because of Kenny Ross that you came to Rowton?"

Jane's coffee turned tasteless in her mouth.

"What — what do you mean?"

He shrugged. "I thought maybe there was something between you two. You acted so odd when I asked about him."

"I'm not involved with anyone," she said quietly, panic subsiding.

"Good," he commented.

"I'm just new at my job and Doug . . . well, he's a bit difficult to handle — "

"You can say that again," Alan said sharply.

"And I'm not used to working in an office," she finished.

"What did you do before?"

"Oh, a bit of this and that, mostly domestic work," she said evasively.

This conversation was becoming dangerous she decided, and very determinedly began to ask Alan about himself. An hour flew by then she said she'd better get home. When they drew up outside her lodgings, Alan stopped the car and turned to look at her.

"I'm glad I saw you tonight, but I'd decided anyway to come back to the garage and speak to you again, Jane."

"Why?" she asked cautiously.

"You're not the type to fish for compliments so you must know the reason. I want to see you again."

Jane felt herself blushing. The thought

was very comforting. But was it fair to Alan? Should she see him again, knowing she was not being honest with him about her real identity, that she was Kenny's sister? She began to undo the safety-belt and open the car door.

"Well, you know where to find me. Thanks for the lift, Alan. Good-night," and she fled into the house.

She sat on her bed for several minutes before taking off her coat, thinking over her evening. That had been a nasty moment when she was leaving the Pretty Puma. Thank goodness Alan had come along when he did. It really was most fortunate. Lucky in fact. A tremendous coincidence.

Or was it? Could he have been following her, just as Doug had done at first? She thought back again to that moment in the office this morning when Doug had sat on her desk blocking her view of Alan Nelson. Shielding her, she'd thought then. What if, in fact, he'd signalled a message to Alan. What if Alan hadn't come round about football at all, but had really been trying to find out Kenny's whereabouts.

Doug could have put him up to it. First of all trying to shock information out of her and when that failed, trying an innocent approach. What if Doug was using Alan to befriend her and that way find out about Kenny?

Oh no, that was too far-fetched. She wanted to trust Alan. He was pleasant and charming in a light-hearted way. She needed his company. She began to feel she'd been hasty and perhaps a little rude in rushing out of his car like that. Maybe he was still outside. Perhaps she should go out and apologise.

She jumped off the bed and ran over to the window, drawing back the curtain a little, but Alan's car had gone.

There was only one car parked outside Mrs Brodie's house. A large black, shiny American car, wings and fins outlined in chrome. The very car that had been parked right outside the Pretty Puma.

It sat outside her room like a great evil black beetle.

5

JANE was adding up a lengthy column of figures when the telephone rang.

"Drat!" She placed her finger at the last figure she'd added and jotted down her total so far on a scrap pad. "Speedwell Services," she said, hoping it would be a quick call.

Immediately she heard the familiar bleeps of a pay-phone. The column of figures was forgotten as both hands gripped the receiver.

"Jane?" the voice at the other end of the line was hesitant.

It was Kenny!

"It's me, is it safe to talk?" he went on quickly.

"Yes, Kenny. Now tell — "

But her brother interrupted her.

"Why are you working at Speedwell?"

"Doug asked me to stay here until

you come back," she told him.

"Oh no," she could hear the groan in Kenny's voice. "Does anyone there know you are my sister?"

"Only Doug. Why?"

"Don't tell anyone there about me, Jane. It's very important. And nobody must know you've heard from me."

"But, Kenny — "

"Look, I'm okay. I just need time to — "

There was a thunderous noise in the background and she lost Kenny's next few words.

"Where are you?" she asked.

"It's better you don't know."

"Are you mad? I must know!"

Again there was noise at his end, repeated bangs and clatters this time.

She caught the words " — can't tell."

"The money, Kenny, I must know about that."

"I didn't steal it."

"Where is it then?"

Someone began shouting at Kenny's

end of the line. She could hardly hear him.

"Jane, don't tell anyone anything, don't talk about me — or the money, if you want to see me again. I've got to go now. I'll keep in touch. Look after yourself, sis," and he rang off before Jane could say another word.

Her first impulse was to burst into tears. What a stupid, frustrating phone call. She was no further forward. She knew precisely nothing. Kenny's whereabouts were still a mystery and where was the money? He said he hadn't stolen it, so who had? Why did he have to stay away then? Why had she to keep quiet about him, and hide the fact that she was his sister?

And why did he sound so scared?

He must have been calling from a phone box without any glass whatsoever, the noises had been terrific. What could have been the words she missed? She tried frantically to remember the sequence of their conversation. She closed her eyes and concentrated, but all was dominated by the noise. There had been something different about it, not ordinary street noises, like cars and buses and passers-by. He had definitely been out of doors, yet there had been an echo quality to the sounds. The first noise had been that thunderous rumble, then bangs, then shouting. And then it struck her — it was so simple. Kenny had been phoning from a railway station! A train had approached and stopped; carriage doors had banged closed and the shouts had been repetitive — the same words in fact . . . or a name. It had registered with her unconsciously.

Desperately Jane pressed her fingertips to her temples in an effort to recall the name. Ex — she could remember that. The name began with an Ex. Exeter? No, the name had been shorter than that, only two syllables. Her eyes flew open and searched round the small office. The place was full of maps and directories. She'd find the place. The AA book caught her eye and she dragged it from the shelf and opened the town index at E. All the 'Exes' were in the south. Surely Kenny hadn't gone that far? But no, none of the names sounded like the one she'd heard.

"Good morning, Jane."

She jumped visibly. "Oh, hello — " she looked up to see Doug regarding her quizzically.

"What's the AA book for?"

"Oh . . . just checking on some mileages."

"Or looking for a suitable place to meet Kenny?" he challenged.

She closed the book with a snap, stood up and looked Doug straight in the eye.

"I don't know where Kenny is," she said, and he would never know how much that truth pained her.

She saw that he believed her.

He shrugged. "OK, let's open the mail. Who knows, he may have sent us a postcard saying 'wish you were here'," he finished sarcastically.

Jane slit the envelopes, scanned the

142

letters and passed them to Doug. He had taken the only other chair in the office. Silently he passed back several letters to her, knowing she was now capable of dealing with them herself.

"Hey — what do you think of this?" he said, waving a distinctive letterheaded paper at her.

"The travel company asking for a regular three-car hire?" She knew he would be interested in that.

"It's quite an idea, Jane. This company suggests I supply three cars, run, service and keep them for their exclusive use, on payment of a very nice regular sum of money." He looked at her thoughtfully. "This could be quite something."

She caught his eye. "I see what you mean. You're guaranteed money monthly so financially it is secure and, if it catches on — "

Doug jumped up and she realised she was seeing a different man. The light of challenge was in his eye and his face was alive with enthusiasm.

"I could build up a fleet of exclusive hire cars. Jane, this could be the big-time for Speedwell Services."

She was cautious. "The only snag is that this — " she consulted the letter again " — Mr Prentice wants to discuss it with you here."

"Snag?"

"Here?" she made an encompassing gesture with one hand.

Slowly Doug's eyes took in the small office with its years of accumulated files, records and catalogues, the dingy carpet, the sale room reject furniture.

"Not exactly the executive image," he admitted ruefully. "Right, I'll soon fix that. We'll clear out these ancient files, strip the walls," he began to unpin maps and notices. "Couple of coats of emulsion — "

"White," said Jane. "Makes the place look bigger."

He smiled at her. "You can help me choose a carpet and a decent desk."

"A typist's chair and an armchair," she suggested quietly.

He laughed. "You'll be putting curtains up on the business window next."

"Don't tempt me," she laughed in return.

"I'll go and think about a reply while I supervise the men. Meanwhile, old Tom can start clearing out in here. Anything dated more than eighteen months ago can go." He left the office whistling.

He left Jane with her mind in a whirl. She, laughing with Doug! What had happened to her? When he'd come into the office she'd been frantic with worry over Kenny. How could she have forgotten her brother so quickly? But she hadn't of course, just for a few moments she'd had something entirely different to think about. And yet she meant what she'd said to Doug. The prospect of brightening up the office, of expanding Speedwell Services, interested her. Somehow she had become involved with the place despite the antagonism between Doug and herself. Maybe she was subconsciously preserving the garage for Kenny's return.

Donning her overall she began to attack the heap of old files scattered about the office. The door opened slightly and Tom sidled into the office. She forced a smile; there was something about the man that she couldn't take to. He was nearly sixty she guessed, the oldest employee Doug had. He had an unhealthy air about him, as if he didn't have enough exercise or fresh air or proper food. Jane knew she should feel sympathetic towards him but it was impossible.

"Hello, Tom, I think we should put this rubbish in dustbin bags straight away. Can you organise that?"

"Sure, Jane, glad to help," Tom smiled easily but his eyes had no warmth in them.

"What's all this in aid of?" he asked a few minutes later as Jane passed him out-of-date papers. "Brightening up things for a welcome return of the prodigal, Kenny Ross?"

Jane kept her control. "The boss didn't say."

"It really amazes me, you know. If anyone else here had taken off like Ross did, the boss would have been fit to be tied," he said.

"Perhaps this Kenny Ross is a good worker."

"Doug tell you that?" Tom asked quickly.

"No," she would not be drawn.

"Seems he's not at his lodgings either. Must've left town."

How did Tom know Kenny wasn't at Mrs Brodie's?

"You seem to know a lot about him, Tom?" she ventured.

"Owes me money, he does, went round to collect it since he hasn't showed up here. Landlady's mouth zipped and padlocked though. That Brodie woman was always close-mouthed."

Jane sent a silent 'thank you' to Mrs Brodie for not letting on that she was living in Kenny's room, and that she was his sister.

"Still, expect he'll be back before long. Need his wages, he will. Never knew a young lad spend money like him."

"Things cost so much these days." Jane tried to sound deliberately vague.

"Doesn't help when you throw it away." Tom stuffed some more files into a bag. "Gambling," he finished quietly.

She kept her face hidden. So he knew about Kenny's gambling too. Did he also know about the Pretty Puma gambling club? It was two days now since she'd been there and she'd been too scared to go back. She still felt icy cold at the memory of that evening — and the fact that someone in that awful black car had followed her home.

Had they only wanted to see who she'd been with? Well, now they knew it was a policeman. She hadn't heard from Alan Nelson since that evening.

Perhaps she'd been too offhand with him and hurt his feelings. She hoped not; she really liked him and she so desperately needed a friend in this town.

But she'd have to go back to the club. It was the only way she could find out more about Kenny. She knew now that the card had been sent to entice her there. She'd walked right into the trap. But what kind of trap was it? They couldn't know about her connection with Kenny. Only Doug and Mrs Brodie knew. And if Mrs Brodie didn't give anything away to Tom, she'd hardly be likely to do so to total strangers. That left Doug.

She'd almost forgotten Tom when he spoke again.

"'Course, maybe Ross has enough money to keep him in luxury for a while."

Still she said nothing, didn't look at Tom, but she was aware he was waiting for an answer.

"Some folks can get lucky at gambling,"

he said eventually.

"I wouldn't know, Tom. I don't believe in it." She straightened up. "That's the lot then, thanks. Take them out to the yard. I'll cope with the rest myself."

He was looking at her, reluctant to go. She opened the office door with a flourish.

"I'll bet you've had enough of this Tom, do go and get some tea."

She left him no option but to leave the office. She made herself some coffee and took five minutes break. She needed it. There was no doubt Tom had been quizzing her about Kenny. Probably he'd been trying to find out what Doug had told her.

Had Kenny borrowed money from Tom for gambling? It looked rather like it. But then there was Tom's remark about Kenny having enough money to keep him in luxury for a while. Was he hinting at a big gambling win? Tom didn't know about the takings, she was certain of that. Doug's pride would never have allowed him to tell his staff that his prize employee, Kenny, had apparently stolen from him.

But the real worry was the fact that Kenny owed Tom money. Were there any others? Perhaps running away had been the only answer for him. The familiar dread began to swamp Jane. Kenny had sounded so young, so honest on the telephone — but he was missing and the money; he did frequent the gambling club and he owed money . . .

Doug came in again and began to discuss with her the reply to be sent to Prentice Travel Agency. When they had finally decided on the wording, Jane began to type it. To her surprise, Doug didn't leave the office.

"By the way, I won't be here on Friday," he said. "It's the Kids' Day Out." He saw her questioning look. "Once a year all the taxi drivers and car hirers in town take underprivileged kids out for the day. Sometimes we go to the seaside, sometimes the Zoo, or for a picnic. We club together and buy them some goodies to eat."

Jane lifted her hands from the typewriter. "What a super idea."

Doug smiled. "Do you know, some of the kids have never seen the sea, or even been in a car?"

"Things we take for granted."

He nodded. "Some of us get as big a kick out of taking them as the kids have being there."

She began typing again, wondering that this hard-headed businessman had any time for children.

"Kenny came with me last year." There was no mistaking the inference in his voice.

"You'd like me to come?" Jane stared at him.

"If you'd drive another car. Speedwell usually provides two cars."

"All right, I'll come."

"Wear something pretty, it's a party."

After he'd left her, Jane could hardly hide a smile. She would wear something pretty, but what about him? Was he going to turn up in his jeans and battered leather jacket, or would he wear his chauffeur's grey suit?

She scarcely recognised him on the Friday morning. He was wearing smart beige and brown checked trousers, a cream wool shirt and a casual brown corduroy jacket.

She was pleased when she saw the approval in his eyes for her skirt and waistcoat ensemble. She'd made it herself, in soft Vyella; the flower-patterned skirt was gathered at the waist, and she'd lined the matching waistcoat with the same material as her blouse. She carried a chunky cardigan in case the day was cold.

The whole garage had joined in preparations for the day. The two cars, the white wedding Cortina and the pale blue one, were decked out with balloons and streamers. Angus and Bert were just putting the finishing touches as Doug and Jane entered the parking area.

"Where is it this year, Doug?" Angus asked.

"Picnic at the Faery Glade. Trees to climb, streams to fall in, cows to chase, so help me," he said with mock fear.

"I feel as if you should put a 'Just Married' sign on the back of my car," Jane said, getting into the driving seat of the blue Cortina.

"Only thing missing is the confetti," Angus laughed.

"We won't forget that on your wedding day, Jane, don't worry," Bert grinned through the windscreen.

Jane smiled back. Wedding day! She wondered briefly if that would ever come. One thing sure, it wouldn't be while she was at Speedwell Services.

The collection point for the children was the Town Square and Jane felt quite moved when she saw the anticipation and wonder on the faces of the children gathered there.

"Right, Jane, we each take four children. You've been allocated — let me see," Doug consulted a long list.

"Susan, Tracy, Bobby and Gavin," he called the children over.

Their ages ranged from six to ten. Jane's heart went out to them. They stood in a row, scrubbed clean, wearing spotless but obvious hand-me-down clothes, but worn with pride. She saw the eyes of the two girls taking in every detail of her outfit, as if memorising it. The boys meanwhile had already started on the crisps for the journey.

It was just like a procession as they left Rowton. The people turned to wave as the gaily decorated taxis and cars passed. The police had obviously been alerted and the route was cleared for them. From time to time Jane glanced in her driving mirror. The four children sat on the edge of the back seat, their eyes swivelling from window to window, as if they were at a tennis match. The only sound was the relentless crunch of crisps. She had tried talking to them, but could get nothing beyond "Yes, miss. No, miss," and realised the children would have to overcome their shyness before real contact was made.

She found to her surprise that Doug was in charge at the Faery Glade. He organised games and races. Since all the other drivers were men, Jane busied herself with the tea urn and setting out the sandwiches and cakes.

Eventually everyone sat down to eat and Doug brought his children over to join Jane's group.

"He says I'm a cissy, going with a woman driver," Gavin pointed at one of the boys with Doug.

"She's the best driver," piped up Susan, in the spirit of women's lib. "And she's the prettiest."

"I'll agree to that," Doug said.

"There's not much competition," Jane laughed, looking round at the stalwart drivers.

There was still a muttered altercation going on between Gavin and the other boy.

Doug swung round. "OK you two, don't spoil it for the others, get me?"

Jane saw the respect in the boys' eyes. "Sorry," they mumbled.

"No hard feelings," Doug said. "Let's have a game of 'beat the goalie' — that's me."

The boys ran off happily with Doug, while Jane and the girls wandered off to pick some flowers. It was the happiest day Jane had had in a long time. It brought back memories of her serene, peaceful life with the Meade family. So much in her life had changed since then. And yet there was a sense of purpose which had been missing before. She hadn't heard from Kenny for two days, but she knew she had to carry on, with optimism and even a little faith.

It was much later when Jane heard the cry, saw a boy lying on the ground and Doug sprinting towards him. When she reached them, Doug was kneeling by the boy's side.

"He's fallen out of the tree. I think he's unconscious. I'll have to fetch a doctor."

Jane quickly took the boy's pulse. "Just a moment, Doug. I think he's only stunned. I'll see if anything is broken. Don't forget, I trained as a nurse."

She looked closely at the boy, noticing his colour was returning. With professional calm she examined his limbs.

"Can I have the First Aid kit from one of the cars, Doug?"

"I'll get it, love," Jane didn't turn round, but recognised the north country accent of Joe, one of the town's regular taxi drivers.

Slowly the boy opened his eyes and saw Doug and Jane.

"Sorry, Mr Doug, shouldn't have climbed that tree. Was just showing off. Me arm hurts like anything."

"OK Mike, take it easy," Doug spoke softly and tore off his cord jacket to pillow it under Mike's head. "Jane's a nurse and she knows what she's doing."

Joe returned with the box and

158

Jane cleaned the gash in Mike's arm and carefully bandaged it, while Doug spoke calmly and encouragingly to him.

"Can we move him?" Doug asked.

"Yes, but I think it would be best if he lies on the back seat of the car. He's had a bit of a shock." She knotted a sling and carefully slipped Mike's arm into it. She said nothing in front of him, but knew the arm would have to be X-rayed at the hospital to make sure there was no fracture.

"OK Tarzan," Doug said. "I'll take you to the car."

With infinite gentleness he lifted Mike and slowly carried him to his own car. Jane helped to make the boy comfortable, all the time quietly impressed with Doug's care. She felt even more admiration for him a few minutes later as he talked to the other children, reassuring them about Mike. There was an attitude about Doug that she hadn't ever seen before. It took her a little while to put a name to it, but eventually she realised it was compassion

"I'm so glad you were here," he said to her as they prepared to leave the Faery Glade.

Impulsively she put her hand on his arm. "It was only an accident, Doug, don't let it mar the day for you. You've been wonderful with the children."

"Funny thing," he squinted at the boys and girls as they shuffled and pushed their way into the numerous cars and taxis. "A cantankerous old bully like me being crazy about kids. We have that at least in common, Jane."

She smiled at him and the look they exchanged seemed to go on for a while, as if suspended above their everyday working relationship, the antagonists for once united. It was a bond between them, but fragile as the web of the spider.

"'appen the lad will be all right now." They looked away from each other as Joe joined them.

"I think so, thanks for your help," Jane smiled at him, but something was tugging at her subconscious. Something that had nothing to do with the picnic, or Mike, but was connected with Joe's accent.

She was just starting the car when it hit her. The dropped 'H'. Lots of people spoke like that. Put an 'H' in front of 'Ex' . . . she had it! The name of the railway station she'd been puzzling over was Hexham! Now she knew where Kenny was! The relief and elation were enormous; she was longing to share that with someone. She looked for Doug, but he was already driving out of the parking area.

She could hardly wait to tell him. Perhaps they could go and find Kenny together. She dismissed entirely her earlier suspicions of Doug. Any man who had such compassion for children as she'd seen today could be trusted to the ends of the earth. She realised that the hard, aggressive Doug of Speedwell Services was only a business front, and the real man cared deeply about people . . . about Kenny. He was protecting him after all!

It was late when they returned to the garage. Together they had taken Mike to Rowton Hospital but an X-ray revealed no damage. Mike returned to the children's home tired, but something of a hero to his pals.

Jane didn't have an opportunity to say anything to Doug about Hexham as he was full of enthusiasm again for the new travel firm venture.

"If this comes off, Jane, I'll feel all the hard work and disappointments throughout the years have been worth-while. I'd like to have the best reputation in Rowton for reliability and service. That means a lot to me."

He drove her home in the Mini and Mrs Brodie had tea and scones ready for them when they arrived. They sat down wearily at the kitchen table.

Now, thought Jane, is the time to tell Doug all she knew about Kenny.

"By the way," Mrs Brodie turned

round as she was leaving the kitchen, "A man came round today to see you, Jane; something about a job. He said — it's yours if you want it."

Jane felt herself tremble. Without looking round at Doug she was aware of the tension in the room.

"What job?" he barked at her.

"A part-time job in the evenings," she said, as calmly as she could.

"Isn't your present job good enough for you? I know I threatened to deduct a sum from your wages to cover the missing money, but you may have noticed that I haven't done so."

"Yes, I noticed," she said quietly. "So I save most of my salary from the garage. This job is an extra insurance against the time when Kenny returns. He . . . he might need money."

"Where is this job?" Doug demanded. "Is it a bar or something like that?"

"Yes, it is a sort of bar."

"Jane, the name, please. Or I'll ask Mrs Brodie. You can bet your last dollar she found out, but I'd rather you told me."

Jane shrugged casually, too casually. "I think it's called the Pretty Puma."

Doug erupted from his chair. "You silly, idiotic girl, that's a gambling club run by Carl Reyburn. A club with the lowest possible reputation in Rowton. You're not taking the job."

Jane leapt up. "I am!"

"I forbid it!"

"*You* forbid it! Who are you to forbid me to do anything?" she shouted.

"Take this job and the deductions start this week."

"Go ahead and deduct. Nothing will stop me from taking this job."

He swung on his heel and stormed out of the house.

Jane walked to the chair where he'd been sitting and picked up his crumpled cord jacket which he'd forgotten. She shook out the creases made when it had been a pillow for Mike. Had that been only a few hours ago?

She supposed she could understand

his anger in a way. She wasn't fooled by Carl Reyburn of the Pretty Puma. She knew it was a sleazy place. But how else could she find out about Kenny if she didn't go? And she could hardly tell Doug that she'd discovered Kenny had been gambling. Now, of course, she couldn't tell him she'd found out Kenny was in Hexham. She sighed; there seemed no comparison at all between the gentle Doug of the picnic and the domineering aggressive man who'd just left her.

She slept badly, her dreams and nightmares a confusion of trains, trees and croupiers. Heavy-eyed she left the house next morning, unaware of much around her.

"Hi — "

She turned to see Alan Nelson waiting on the pavement.

"Hello, Alan." She was genuinely pleased to see him. Obviously he had not taken offence at her rather abrupt goodnight a few evenings ago.

"My chariot awaits, if you'd like a lift

to work," he gestured to his car parked by the kerbside. "I'm going your way."

"I'd really appreciate that, I'm rather late as it is," she smiled and slipped into the passenger seat.

They conversed easily and exchanged a bit of banter and she began to relax again. He was a most attractive man and so pleasant to be with that it was very easy to agree to go out with him the following Saturday.

To her surprise, and consternation, he walked right into the garage with her.

Doug was already in the office, opening the mail.

"Good morning, Jane," he said pleasantly, and she had the instant impression that he was sorry about his outburst the previous evening. "You're early."

"Yes, Alan gave me a lift." She stepped into the office and then Alan was clearly visible to Doug.

Doug's face settled in its grim lines when he saw the constable.

"Thanks," he said brusquely, nodding at Alan. "We can get started now. We're busy."

It was an obvious dismissal and once again Jane was wary. Why did Doug want her to have nothing to do with Alan? What exactly had he told the police about Kenny, if anything?

She turned to Alan and smiled. "I'll see you as arranged."

"Actually, I'm here on official business," he replied coolly.

Jane's coat seemed to weigh a ton as she tried to slip it off her shoulders.

"Oh?" Doug's voice was clipped.

"A cash box has been found," Alan said, then looked a little surprised as both Jane and Doug stared at him, without replying.

"And?" Doug said eventually.

"And it has the initials SS on the side, similar in design to the sign above your garage. Have you lost a cash box recently?"

Doug ignored the veil of sarcasm in Alan's tone.

"Yes, as a matter of fact, I mislaid one."

"You didn't report its loss."

Doug shrugged carelessly. "Not really a loss, constable, you understand. As I said, I mislaid it."

"I'll get it from the car, perhaps you will be able to identify it." Alan left the office.

Jane hung up her coat with trembling hands, then turned to Doug.

"Is it your cash box?"

"I expect so."

"Did it go missing on the day that Kenny left?"

"Yes."

"You didn't tell me before."

Doug looked at her but didn't reply.

"You haven't told me everything, have you?" she said accusingly.

"That makes us square, doesn't it, Jane," he retorted.

She caught her breath. How near she had been yesterday to telling him all about Kenny. How much more was this man concealing from her?

Alan returned to the office carrying the grey metal box. The Speedwell Services sign was printed on the side.

"Yes, that's mine," Doug said without hesitation.

"Perhaps you can tell us what it contains, Mr Evans," Alan said.

"Why?"

"To confirm identification."

Jane's hands were clammy with fear. If the cash box contained the missing thousand pounds then Kenny was in the clear. But if it did, how was Doug going to explain that he'd 'mislaid' a cash box containing that amount of money?

"Haven't you inspected the contents?" Doug asked.

"We couldn't get it open. Do you have a key?"

Doug put his hand in his pocket and withdrew a small metal key. He inserted it in the lock.

Calmly Alan Nelson put his hand firmly on the lid.

"Before you open it, Mr Evans, I'd

like to know what it contains."

"Some savings of mine . . . can't say how much exactly. Don't tell me it's a silly thing to do, constable. I know it. That's why I felt such a fool when I mislaid the box. Me, the self-made man of Rowton, not keeping my money in the bank."

Despite her tension, Jane could only marvel at Doug's glib reply. Silently she prayed the box held all his money; that it held proof of her brother's innocence.

Alan Nelson lifted his hand.

"All right, Mr Evans. Open the box."

6

WITH studied casualness, Doug inserted his key into the lock, turned it and slowly raised the lid. He hadn't once looked in her direction but Jane knew he was very much aware of her anxiety. She had unconsciously moved nearer to the two men, so when the box was finally opened she too could see inside.

And, like them, she saw nothing. The cash box was empty.

"Well, you can't win 'em all," Doug shrugged.

Jane hardly heard his throw-away line. No money. Surely that put the stamp of guilt on Kenny. Slowly she turned away, her heart sick. There was nowhere to run to in the small office, no corner to hide. She felt desperate to be out and away from the inescapable truth. She opened the small window and stared across the yard and the street beyond, not seeing people or cars, or anything for that matter. Her thoughts were far away and her mind's eye showed her Kenny, alone and scared, in possession of all that money which wasn't his. For the first time, she admitted to herself that even in the worst moments she'd never really believed Kenny to be guilty.

"You don't seem to be very upset, Mr Evans."

Jane heard Alan's voice behind her.

"It has taught me a lesson, constable. As I said, the bank is the only place for savings," Doug replied.

"Can you say if this cash box was stolen from your home or," Alan paused, " — or from this office?"

Jane closed the window and returned to her desk. There was no way now that Doug could avoid telling Alan the truth about the cash box and Kenny.

"I didn't say it was stolen."

"Pardon me, I remember now, you said 'mislaid'."

"Precisely, constable, that is why I didn't report its loss. Nor do I want this business carried any further."

Jane sat very still. Doug was still not exposing Kenny.

She became aware of the electric atmosphere in the office. Doug and Alan were tensely staring as if ready to lunge at each other.

"In that case, I'm wasting my time," Alan said tightly.

"Sorry, constable, it was good of you to return the cash box. I'll be more careful next time." Doug tried to sound placating, but the result was false.

"Right," Alan then turned to Jane. "Cheerio just now. I'll be in touch." He gave her a small, tight smile.

He stopped as he reached the door. "And Kenny Ross?" he asked Doug.

The air seemed to spark with tension.

"What about him?"

"That's my question," Alan persisted. "What about Kenny?"

Doug stared at him, evidently unable

to think of a reply.

Alan sighed impatiently. "Any word of him, or when he's planning to return to Rowton?"

Jane fixed her eyes on the typewriter. She couldn't bear to look at either man.

"Not yet. As I said last time, we'll let you know when he's back," Doug said.

Alan didn't reply, just closed the door behind him and went away.

Doug flung himself into the chair and sat staring at the floor for a long time. Jane watched him, unable to think of anything to say. It looked like the end of everything though.

"There were two keys to this cash box," Doug began to speak very quietly. "I had one, Cathie Johnson the other, which I presume she handed over to Kenny when she became ill. Since the box is empty and the lock hasn't been forced, it's logical to assume that whoever had the other key now has the money." He paused. "Wouldn't you agree, Jane?" His voice was calm, almost gentle as he asked the question.

"Yes."

"I had been hoping that this box would be found with the money intact. That perhaps someone had stolen it from Kenny and that he'd been afraid to come back here."

"I'd been hoping that too," she said.

"Kenny must have the money, Jane. He must have taken it. Why? He didn't need to steal from me. If he needed more money all he had to do was ask me. We had a good working relationship — or so I thought. I'm not an unreasonable man." Doug got up again and paced the small floor area of the office, his fists jammed in his pockets.

"OK let's assume that he has the money. Maybe he's spent some of it — but surely he can't have spent the entire thousand pounds!" He looked at Jane in appeal.

She shook her head. Surely not, she prayed.

"He wasn't one for spending money," Doug went on. "At least not foolishly. He didn't smoke, or drink. I guessed that Cathie was his girlfriend but she's a quiet kid. I don't reckon they lived it up. Cathie's the type who would prefer saving up to get married and there's nothing wrong in that. So why did he need the money, Jane? Why? Is there something I don't know about?"

She couldn't look Doug straight in the eye and lie at the same time. She wouldn't have done that with anyone. But she didn't tell him about Kenny's connection with the gambling club and that Tom claimed Kenny owed him money.

She shrugged . . . "I don't know."

He leant his hands on her desk and stared at her.

"You must know something! You've been in touch with Kenny — don't deny it. You're not the type of person to let this situation rest. I know you well enough by now. You will have been doing everything possible to clear it up. Let's work on this together now. What has Kenny told you?"

"Nothing — " She spread her hands to emphasise the word.

Doug's short temper erupted again.

"Oh, for goodness sake Jane, what is the matter with you? Right — I'm giving him, and you, one last chance. Tell him to come home, with the money, or whatever is left of it. Otherwise, I'll do something about this — something he won't like and you won't like. You do realise that by shielding him, Jane, you could be accused of being an accessory after the fact?" He left the office.

She slumped in her chair. She wouldn't have believed that this situation could get any worse. One last chance. She'd have to insist that Kenny came home now.

She really ought to be grateful to Doug for this last chance. And yet, why didn't he act now? Why another chance for Kenny? Doug had had the opportunity to have the whole matter cleared up with Alan's arrival with the cash box. He now had proof that Kenny had taken the money. No one else could have taken it, only Kenny had the duplicate key.

What other business man, especially one so similar in outlook to Doug, would act in this way? The tiny seed of suspicion that Jane had been nursing since she first met Doug resurfaced. There was something that didn't ring true about his attitude. He admitted that he hadn't told her everything. The cash box was a good example. She was convinced that he knew more about this mystery than he was telling her.

He wanted Kenny back, but still without the police knowing anything about it. Therefore, there must be something that he wanted to keep from them.

She thought about Kenny again. He had never actually said that he didn't have the money — only that he didn't steal it. There was no way round it; Kenny had to come home. She wanted to sort this out with him before either Doug or the police got on to it. She must try to persuade Kenny to return secretly, or to meet her somewhere.

On a sudden impulse she picked up the telephone and dialled Cathie Johnson's number.

"Did Kenny phone you last night?" she asked the girl.

"No," Cathie said.

"Good," Jane said, not realising she sounded a little heartless. "That means he'll phone today. Tell him he *must* phone me."

"At the office?" Cathie was horrified.

"Yes," she said grimly. "I'll try to come and see you tonight, anyway."

"Come for tea, Jane. I'd love to see you again," Cathie said.

But the first telephone call that came through for her was far more frightening.

"Carl Reyburn here, Miss Mitchell," the quiet voice spoke in her ear.

Jane nearly dropped the receiver. "Mr Reyburn, you have no right to phone me at this office," she said angrily.

"My apologies, but I have been hoping to see you at the Pretty Puma."

"Yes, yes. I got your message. I will be round about the job," she said hurriedly, terrified in case Doug should walk into the office. He'd been furious when he'd heard about the job.

"Make it tonight, Miss Mitchell. I pay well and good jobs are hard to find." He hung up.

Jane banged down the receiver. How she hated supercilious people. For two pins she'd tell him what to do with his job. Then reason prevailed and she acknowledged to herself that she simply had to take it. She had to find out exactly what Kenny had been doing at the club and if he had gambling debts, as Tom had hinted. But she didn't like Carl Reyburn phoning her at the office. She didn't like it at all.

She heard footsteps approaching the

office door and instantly straightened up, making a tremendous effort to appear normal. Doug came in, sat down and immediately began to talk business, as if the morning's episode with Alan Nelson had not happened. For a moment Jane was taken aback, then realised that it was the only way to behave. Life had to go on. If she didn't keep to a routine, too, she would break down completely.

"About this new contract with the Prentice Travel Agency, Jane — there are quite a number of details to be worked out. We don't have time during the day, so could you possibly help out one evening?"

"I'm not sure — " she began, thinking of her invitation to Cathie's and her later appointment at the Pretty Puma.

Doug's face closed. "Forget it. I just thought you might have some ideas."

"I have," she said calmly. Despite the topsy-turvy state of life, and the fact that she'd been more or less blackmailed into a job she'd never tackled in her life before, she found she was enjoying the challenge at Speedwell Services. "I've been invited to Cathie's for tea tonight, but — "

"I could pick you up from there, say about eight?" he suggested quickly.

Eight would be ideal, thought Jane swiftly. When Kenny phoned it was always around seven in the evening. If he didn't phone her before she left the office, she would be able to speak to him at Cathie's.

"Right, that will do fine."

"Thanks," he said, and left again.

At last Jane began her work for the day, but her mind was busily planning the evening. Surely Doug wouldn't expect her to work more than a couple of hours. If she left the garage at ten, she could easily make her way to the Pretty Puma in time. Clubs like that stayed open well into the small hours. Pleased that her plans were well formulated, Jane felt considerably cheered.

But she was too late at Cathie's. Kenny had already phoned.

"He says it's difficult to phone during the day," Cathie told her. "But he will speak to you soon."

She related all that Kenny had said but, as Jane expected, nothing was important. She knew that Kenny wouldn't tell his girlfriend anything about the money, or his fears. Jane also suspected that he wasn't too keen to speak to *her*, knowing she'd try to persuade him to come home. But he didn't know about the latest development.

"Was it a bad line?" she asked Cathie.

"Yes, how did you know that? Do you think there's something wrong with our telephone — it happens every time?"

"No, it's probably just because he's phoning from a distance," Jane said.

"I wish I knew where he was," Cathie was wistful.

Jane didn't reply but she was beginning

to suspect that Kenny phoned from the same call box every time. And it wasn't necessarily a bad line — just a noisy background. Railway station noises. Kenny must be working near Hexham railway station. The knowledge comforted Jane a little.

Doug arrived promptly at eight to collect her. To her surprise he didn't head in the direction of the garage.

"I have the painters in the office tonight, only time they could come. So, if you don't object, I thought we could work at my place."

"Oh," the dismay in her voice was obvious. How would she get to the club?

"Don't worry, you'll be quite safe with me," he said dryly.

She couldn't say that that wasn't what was worrying her and she daren't tell him what was.

"Good." She tried to shrug off the implication as casually as possible.

She hadn't thought at all about Doug's private life and so she was rather surprised when she saw where he lived. His home was the top floor of a Victorian terrace house with a rather grand entrance. They went up a sweeping staircase to the last landing where there was a narrow private door to Doug's flat. A steep staircase led to the top floor.

"No prizes for guessing that this used to be the servants' quarters when this was a family home," he told her. "They had three small rooms at the back of the house. I've converted two into a kitchen and bathroom and the third makes an ideal bedroom."

He led her along a narrow landing.

"This, on the other hand, makes up for everything. The former billiards room."

They went into a long room at the front of the house. It had a beautifully panelled ceiling, two small dormer windows giving magnificent views of the hills that surrounded Rowton, and a large cupola in the centre of the ceiling spilled in some extra light.

Doug had divided the room into dining and living areas. Both had natural pine furnishings and the upholstery, walls and carpeting were soft muted shades of oatmeal and yellow and russet. The whole effect was relaxing and peaceful and pleasing to the eye.

Doug had disappeared to make coffee so she had time to wander around looking at his books, his paintings, and some pieces of pottery which were scattered about shelves and tables.

So this was the private Doug Evans. She was frankly stunned.

She had no opportunity to say anything to him as he was totally businesslike when he returned with the coffee. They sat at the dining table and set to work immediately. It was a difficult task to cost the new venture and they discovered snag after snag. But Jane was engrossed in the work and amazed when Doug called a halt.

"We still have a great deal to do," she pointed out.

"It is eleven-thirty."

"Oh no!" She remembered about the Pretty Puma.

"It's all right, Cinderella, I'll have you home by midnight. Mrs Brodie won't have locked you out."

Jane sat silent in Doug's car on the way home. There was no way she could get to the gambling club that night. All public transport had stopped in Rowton by this time and she'd only make Mrs Brodie suspicious if she called a taxi at this hour.

Next morning there was a hand-delivered note for her from Carl Reyburn.

"You didn't come last night as promised. Will expect you this evening," it read.

Jane tore it up. She had quite enough on her plate without this man needling her.

However, a pleasant surprise awaited her at the Speedwell Services office. The painters had made a good job and the dingy room was transformed into a bright, cheerful working area. It even looked bigger.

"We'll take some time off today," Doug told her. "After we've made our usual call at the bank, you can help me choose some new furniture for here."

"You don't need my help. After seeing your flat I'd trust your taste implicitly," she told him with a smile.

His face lightened with pleasure at her remark and she reflected that if he didn't have such a grim personality he would be a most attractive man.

"Thanks, but I'd still like you along — the woman's touch, you understand?"

"All right," she agreed equably.

She wondered later if there had been a woman to help him choose his flat furnishings. Now that she came to think of it, she'd never seen him with a girl, or even heard him speak of one. Perhaps there had been no time in his life for love. Surely no career was worth that.

Nevertheless she was impressed by

the attention they were given at all the stores, and the assurance of prompt delivery of all items. Not only was Doug well known in town but obviously he was respected too. Every single item of office furniture was replaced and Jane was thrilled with a new typewriter.

"This might even inspire me to take typing lessons," she told Doug.

"I hope so. I think Speedwell Services is just about to become the biggest thing in this town," he said. "And you know, I never thought you'd stick this job, but you've turned out to be quite an asset."

She laughed. "I could never have imagined myself in an office. The prospect never appealed to me. And yet," she shrugged. "I can't explain it, but as a job it's not at all bad."

She was thoughtful as they drove back to the garage. Just how long did Doug expect her to work for him? For instance, what would happen when Kenny came back? Would he still want her then? She couldn't see him employing Kenny again after all this trouble.

That evening they spent working in his flat again, finalising the details of the new contract. Once again it was late when they finished and she had no opportunity to phone Carl Reyburn to explain. However, the next day was Friday and she'd definitely go then. No doubt that would be one of the club's busier nights, anyway.

"Jane, may I take you out to dinner tomorrow night as a thank-you for your help with this contract?" Doug asked her as they arrived back at her lodgings.

She thought swiftly. She was on dangerous ground. She couldn't tell him about Carl Reyburn's persistent approaches.

"That would be lovely, Doug, but could we make it some night next week? I'll have to catch up on my beauty routine."

"What about Saturday, then?" he asked.

"Oh — I'm already going out." She was embarrassed.

"With that Alan Nelson?"

"Yes."

She thought he was going to make some nasty comment about him but he said nothing for a moment.

"I promised Mike I'd take him out on Sunday," he told her.

"How is he?" she asked, remembering the intrepid little boy at the picnic.

"He's fine now. Maybe you'd come on Sunday, too? I know he'd love that. He asked for you when I saw him the other day."

"Yes, I'd love to come," she agreed.

Next morning, on her way to the garage, a sickeningly familiar car drew up beside her, the big American car she'd nicknamed the 'black beetle'. Carl Reyburn's assistant, the heavy pugilist type, stepped out of it and blocked her path.

"Mr Reyburn's getting impatient," he said, expressionlessly.

"Tell him I've been working late and

haven't been free. I'll definitely be there tonight," she told him angrily.

She walked on to the office but her knees were trembling. There was no doubt that Carl Reyburn was hounding her. He knew where she lived, who she worked for, when to find her. She closed her eyes in brief prayer: "Please, Kenny, phone — and listen to me this time".

But he wouldn't. It was lunchtime on Friday when he rang and at once she recognised the echoing noisy background of the station.

"The police found the cash box," she told him.

"Oh no!"

She heard the panic in his voice.

"Did they take fingerprints and get a description of me from Doug?"

"He didn't give you away. He said he didn't want any investigation made. But he told me to tell you to come back at once!"

"Jane! I told you not to tell him I'd phoned."

"He isn't stupid. He's guessed you've been in touch with me. Please, please come home. You must. The sooner you come home, the better it will be for you."

"No, I can't, not yet. You don't understand that there's more to it — "

"WHAT?"

"Get yourself out of that office, Jane. Away. I don't like you being there. Go back to Ashburn. Anywhere, just get away. I'll come back, but not yet. I'll face up to things when I'm ready. I can't talk any longer now. I know you don't understand, but I do care about you and I don't want you hurt. Leave Rowton now, please love," — he was gone.

Jane felt as though she'd hate the telephone for the rest of her life. She and Kenny never seemed able to converse with any satisfactory result. In fact, every telephone call only served to complicate things even further.

She disregarded his warnings about leaving Rowton and the garage. He had no idea how deeply she was involved with the job nor did he realise that she wanted to see this through. Presumably he wanted her out of the way to prevent Doug threatening and harassing her. Well, she wasn't going to let Doug worry her. She was here to the end, bitter or not.

That evening she walked to Rowton town centre and from there took a bus to the gambling club. She was in a somewhat truculent mood, which was unusual for her, but it served her well in her dealings with Carl Reyburn and she offered no apologies for not going sooner to his club.

She was shown to a small office reached only through Reyburn's room. Her job was simple book-keeping and she wondered why he needed someone to help out. Any other employee, such as the cloakroom girl, could have done the work in odd minutes.

They had agreed she would work for four hours, seven to eleven, on evenings which suited her. She had decided right from the start that she would only stay as long as it took her to find out what Kenny had been doing at the club, but she had to pretend to Carl Reyburn that she was serious about the job.

She worked steadily until about nine-thirty when he came into the office.

"Time for a break, Miss Mitchell. Come and see round my establishment."

Jane tried not to show her eagerness. Now maybe she could begin to find out something.

The Pretty Puma had at one time been a private dwelling house. Reyburn had not made many changes. There was no large gaming area. Each room had been left intact and each was given over to one game — roulette, chemin de fer, etc. Jane guessed he could keep a closer eye on his clients in this way.

"Like to play?" he asked as they stood by the roulette table.

"No thanks," Jane said, covertly looking around to see if there was anyone of Kenny's age playing, anyone he might have struck up a friendship with.

"On the house," Carl Reyburn's voice was smoothly persistent.

"I don't believe in gambling," she said flatly.

"Really? You amaze me, I was so certain — "

"Certain of what?" She looked at the small, neat man with his deceptively mild manner.

"Certain that you would be like your . . . shall we say, predecessor?"

She couldn't answer. She had a premonition of what was coming.

"Kenny Ross." Again the mild smile.

"Who?" she said vaguely.

"Come now, Miss Mitchell. You live at his digs, work in the same place. You came running when I sent you my card. I thought you might have the same luck as Ross — or should I say the same bad luck?"

"I didn't come to play games, Mr Reyburn, just to work. Excuse me, I'll get back to my book-keeping."

She sat with her head down working for the rest of the evening, but her mind was busy. She was going to have to be very careful here. This man was clever; she couldn't afford to take him for a fool. He knew there was a connection between her and Kenny, but he didn't know what it was; that was her trump card at the moment. There was no doubt he would make things as difficult for her as possible, watch her like a hawk to see just what game she was playing. She wasn't scared of him, though. He'd do nothing to harm her, he was too clever for that. There was, however, something else he hadn't reckoned on — her determination to protect her brother.

The week had been so fraught that only the prospect of her date with Alan Nelson on Saturday evening had kept Jane going. She was determined to forget everything and just enjoy herself. He was fun, he was kind, he was attractive and he liked her.

It was a long time since there had been anyone in Jane's life — almost two years in fact, when she'd fallen for a doctor in the hospital where she worked. It hadn't worked out but she hadn't broken her heart. However, it was rather pleasant to be 'courted' again.

Alan took her first to a play at the local theatre. To her delight it was a comedy and her spirits were high as they left the theatre for a small restaurant on the banks of the River Row.

As Alan ordered their meal, she wished that she'd come to Rowton in different circumstances and that she could be open and frank with Alan, that their relationship could get off to an honest start at least. He didn't even know her real name yet. Would he understand when she finally told him everything?

"Jane, why are you working for Doug Evans?" he asked her, abruptly interrupting her thoughts.

"Well . . . it's a well-paid job," she said vaguely.

"Oh, come on, that garage is not your scene at all. You could easily get another secretarial post in a decent office."

She said nothing. To admit she was not a secretary, had not even rudimentary typing skill, would leave her open to more searching questions.

"And a decent man to work for," Alan added.

"What's wrong with Doug Evans? What have you heard?"

He looked at her in surprise.

"Nothing. He seems to be straight as a die, but — "

"But what?" she insisted.

"Well, frankly, don't you think there's something odd about this Kenny Ross business? Do you think he's got rid of him or something?"

"Don't be ridiculous." Her laugh sounded shrill.

"I'm not being ridiculous. Only Evans seems to know where the boy is. No-one else. And what about the sister?"

"What about her?" Jane said warily.

"If Kenny Ross was your brother, wouldn't you want to know where he was?"

"Yes," she admitted. "But maybe the sister does know."

"You mean that Doug Evans has fobbed her off too, with vague excuses?"

Jane shrugged.

"He's certainly made some impression on you," Alan said bitterly.

"What do you mean?"

"He can do no wrong in your eyes, can he? What has he got — scruffy office, couldn't-care-less attitude about his staff. Tell me, Jane, what is his magic charm?"

"He certainly doesn't have charm, Alan. I admit he's short-tempered and a bit abrupt, but he's had a tough time building up that business and I'm sure he wouldn't do anyone any harm." She tried to sound casual. She didn't want Alan taking any further interest in Doug or Kenny.

"Spoken like a trusting, loyal employee. There aren't many of you left and he knows it. The perfect cover for him."

"What does that mean?"

"Nothing for you to worry about, Jane." He took her hand. "I don't like him, I don't like you working for him, and I don't like his attitude over Kenny Ross. Don't worry, you'll be okay and Doug Evans will never know I'm after him."

The whole evening had suddenly gone wrong and she could hardly wait to get home. If Alan really began investigating he'd soon find out she was Kenny's sister and then all the rest. How would he feel about a girl whose brother was a thief?

By one of those odd contrasts the following day, Sunday, spent with Doug and Mike, was perfect. They went to the seaside and they built sandcastles with turrets and moats and carried buckets of water from the sea. They played hide and seek in the sand dunes and ate ice creams and cockles and chips, although not all at the same time.

Mike was in seventh heaven, and she had a strong suspicion that Doug was too. She knew that whatever happened in the future, she'd hold that day, cameo-like, in her heart as one of the most special in her whole life.

There was something about children that seemed to unite herself and Doug. She certainly saw a different side to him. He was a man she could understand, talk, laugh with. There was no awkwardness, no sarcasms, no jibes. Just pure happy, uncomplicated friendship. She wondered yet again what it would have been like to come to Rowton under different circumstances and whether she and Doug could have been friends then, too.

Next weekend was a long holiday, Friday until Tuesday, and Doug made one or two casual references to it during the day. She knew he was hinting that they might take Mike out again over the holiday, but she didn't commit herself to anything. Alan had also asked to see her over the weekend, but perhaps she shouldn't get personally involved with either of them any further.

The new office furniture arrived at the beginning of the week and Jane was thrilled with the new look of Speedwell Services. The travel agency representative came to look round all the premises, not only the office, and he was satisfied with everything.

Doug came into the office later, looking pleased.

"We've pulled it off, Jane. The contract is ours." He looked round the office. "Mind you, I've sunk a lot of capital into this. If anything goes wrong, I could be in big trouble." He paused. "I'm not getting at you, Jane, but I do need the money that Kenny has. Have you told him yet?"

"Yes . . . no." If she told him that Kenny had refused to come back, would he then put the police on to it? She hadn't dared tell him that Alan Nelson was going to investigate *him*.

"Which is it, Jane?"

"I've told him to come back and he's coming, Doug. It's just that I can't pin him down to a date."

"Just make it the end of this week, Jane. OK?"

His voice was quiet and she knew he didn't want to spoil the memory of their day together last Sunday, but she was in no doubt that he meant the end of this week, not next or the next again. Could she, on the strength of their closer friendship, tell him that she was sure Kenny was in Hexham and ask him for advice?

"I'm sure you wouldn't like Alan Nelson put on the case," he said pointedly, going out of the door.

His words hit her like water thrown from a bucket. Her longing to confide in him froze at once. She'd never tell him about Hexham now.

Kenny hadn't phoned her. She was certain he was avoiding speaking to her although he'd rung Cathie almost every evening.

Jane went again to the Pretty Puma that evening, determined to make contact with some of the customers. But it was impossible to stay in the gaming rooms without gambling, so she decided to make a start by chatting first to the cloakroom lady and then the barman. But they didn't know anything — or if they did, they weren't saying.

It wasn't until she was leaving that Carl Reyburn spoke to her.

"If you want to know anything about Kenny Ross, ask me. I can tell you plenty."

She shrugged. "It doesn't matter. I thought I'd try to find out something about the mystery man, but it isn't important."

The smile left Reyburn's face and she could see the harsh, cold lines of his jaw.

"There's no mystery, and it is important, Miss Mitchell. Ross has run away — disappeared. And I want to see him. I have contacts all over the country, of course, and I may have to resort to them." He opened the front door of the club for her. "Unless you help."

As she stepped out into the black Rowton night, he spoke again.

"The choice is yours, Miss Mitchell. Will you give Ross the message, or do I have to send someone else?"

7

SHE needed a car. Although she was surrounded by cars here at Speedwell Services and Doug would certainly have given her the use of one, that was completely out of the question. No one must even suspect that she wanted a car. There was another car-hire company in Rowton, which she would have to visit secretly.

She would, of course, have to give her real name and produce her driving licence, but she must reach the office unobserved by anyone she knew in Rowton. She needed, as they said in the best spy novels, a 'cover'.

Looking round the small, ordinary business office of Speedwell Services, she wondered if this was really happening to her. It was becoming ridiculous. It wasn't as if she was the quarry of some desperate men, but it appeared that Kenny was. She was the contact with the quarry. Kenny was being hunted by Doug, by Carl Reyburn and no doubt by Alan Nelson once he got a hint of the truth. The hunters were closing in.

She'd failed to make Kenny understand that he must return to Rowton of his own free will. There was now no alternative; she had to fetch him home. She wanted to do this secretly as it was imperative she had all the facts of the situation to enable her to handle it. Kenny obviously didn't know where to turn.

Jane decided that her only hope of finding him was to go to the station at Hexham and try to spot him. She'd been laying her plans for two days now; memorising the route to Hexham, dropping hints to Mrs Brodie that she would be away. Tomorrow was Friday, the beginning of the long holiday weekend.

"Good morning, Jane," Doug swept into the office. "Looks like the fine weather will hold over the weekend. Could be perfect for a picnic. How about coming along with Mike and me?"

"Sorry, I just can't make it, Doug."

"Going away?"

She'd thought about this too. Partial honesty might deceive Doug into leaving her alone.

"Yes."

"To see Kenny?"

"I hope to."

"Where?"

"Since he hasn't told me where he is, I think we'll have to meet somewhere. A place we both know."

Doug fell into the trap. "I see, your home town, Ashburn."

She smiled. "You know, I haven't visited Ashburn since I started work here."

He looked at her for a moment. "That's true. You've done nothing but work and worry about that brother of yours since you came here. You deserve a break, Jane. Try to get some fresh air and rest while you're away."

"I will."

"Say, why don't you take one of the cars — no charge."

"Thanks, but no. The bus service is pretty good to Ashburn."

"OK. I'll look forward to seeing you back here on Tuesday." He paused. "With Kenny." He walked away from her.

The sting in the tail; Doug never missed it. Just when she thought things were going well, he'd produce the barb. She always felt absurdly upset, but it didn't matter this time; or she wouldn't allow it to matter. The important thing was that Doug assumed she was going to Ashburn to see Kenny. She knew he wouldn't interfere. He'd let her handle this, at least over the weekend. She read his reasoning — Ashburn was only forty miles away, near enough for him to find Kenny if she was unsuccessful in bringing him back.

She looked up. He was still standing by the door, watching her.

"Jane, if you need any help . . . if you should want me there . . . for anything, just call me." He left.

Her hands were trembling. There had been no strings to that offer. There had been genuine concern and sincerity in his voice. Every instinct in her cried out to accept. Heaven knew she was scared, scared of what Kenny would tell her and of the outcome. But most of all she was scared of having to cope alone. She desperately needed someone strong to advise her, to talk to, to lean on, but how could she be sure that Doug was the right one?

There was Alan Nelson, of course, but she couldn't suddenly confess the whole story to him. She knew Alan's conscience wouldn't allow him to keep quiet about an apparent robbery. No, she had to deceive Alan yet again, but surely this would be the last time.

"I'm spending the weekend with a relative, in the country," she told him when he telephoned an hour later.

"I see." She could hear the disappointment in his voice and that was flattering. "Perhaps I could drive you there?"

"No thanks, Alan. We have all the arrangements tied up. I'll probably see you next week."

"Sure thing, Jane. Enjoy yourself."

How she hated behaving like this. And yet she hadn't lied to Doug, or Alan. She hadn't said she was going to Ashburn, Doug had assumed it. And she was spending the weekend with a relative — Kenny. She just hadn't told Alan which relative. Her thoughts jumped to the following Tuesday. Could she hope that everything would be in the open by then? That she could settle down and enjoy her new job here at Speedwell Services, and have an uncomplicated friendship with Alan?

She had arranged to meet Cathie Johnson for lunch. At one time her plan had been to tell no one that she was going to Kenny, but then she realised she needed Cathie's help.

Kenny was bound to telephone his girlfriend either on the Thursday or Friday. Cathie could give him the message that Jane would be waiting to meet him at Hexham Station.

Over a salad lunch in one of the town's cafes, Jane quickly briefed Cathie. The girl listened patiently, then burst out:

"Jane, let me come to Hexham with you. I'm longing to see Kenny again."

"I'm sorry, Cathie, but it's just too d . . ." she stopped short. She'd been about to say 'dangerous'. " — difficult. Just think, I might miss him at first. I need you here, at the end of your telephone. You'll be doing more for Kenny by being here — being the link between the three of us."

"I suppose you're right. I guess I can wait another few days to see him again."

Jane grinned. "Anyway, he'd never forgive me if I took you along — you're much too precious to him. But I need your help now, too. I have to rent a car

213

from Jones Self-Drive, and I want to be as inconspicuous as possible. Will you come with me to make it look like an innocent shopping trip?"

Cathie gulped the rest of her coffee. "I know the staff entrance to Jones's place. We can slip out of the back of Woolworth's, across the alley and no one will notice."

"Great!"

As they strolled through Woolworth's, Cathie asked her about her journey to Hexham.

"I plan to leave first thing tomorrow morning," Jane told her.

Cathie stopped and gazed at some giant packets of soap powder, but all the time she was speaking to Jane, outlining a few ideas of her own. Then they quickly moved out of Woolworth's.

Even Jane was surprised by Cathie's ingenuity. Within fifteen minutes, they'd traversed the High Street, slipped into Jones Self-Drive, made the booking, and were innocently choosing lipsticks in Boots. If anyone was watching, they looked like two girls spending holiday money.

"Now, Jane, I want you to promise that you will ring me too," Cathie said as Jane prepared to return to the office. "If I'm the one who has to stay behind, I must know exactly what is happening. I don't want you disappearing from my sight too."

Jane was secretly surprised at this new side to Cathie's character. Gone was the helpless little female image; determination was the dominating feature now. If anything proved her love for Kenny, this was it.

She returned to the office in a more optimistic frame of mind. She was no longer alone; she had Cathie. Cathie, staying at home, but being as steady as an anchor. Who would have thought that she could come up with such an ingenious plan for Jane's 'getaway'?

Just before she finished work for the day the older mechanic, Tom, came into the office for a chat. He did this often, claiming he needed a rest, but Jane privately thought he was bone lazy.

"Making the most of the weekend then, Jane? Where is it this time — Majorca, Paris?"

"Actually, Tom, I thought I'd try Miami Beach for a change," she said, forcing gaiety.

"Wishful thinking, if you ask me. Where are you really going?"

An indefinable tension made Jane hesitate. She'd been about to say Ashburn, but instead she made her reply even more vague.

"Where the fancy takes me. I think I'll just wander around seeing the beautiful countryside."

Tom muttered something about 'a nice time', then left the office.

Jane finished her work promptly and was back in her lodgings in time for the evening meal. Her work at the Pretty Puma was over. She realised that she'd only been hired by Carl Reyburn to lead him to Kenny. She was still certain, however, that he was unaware of the relationship between her and Kenny.

Mrs Brodie put a succulent casserole in front of her.

"You need a good solid meal, if you're off travelling tomorrow," her landlady said. "Countryside will be a right change for you after all this time in a dirty town. Mebbe you'll not want to come back."

Jane looked up from her plate. Had she detected a note of regret in Mrs Brodie's voice?

"I never thought I'd take to Rowton, but I have," she said. "I'll be back." All Mrs Brodie said was "fine", but Jane knew she'd been right. Her landlady wanted her back; she was rather touched. "And I hope to bring Kenny with me."

Mrs Brodie sat down opposite her, her stern face thoughtful.

"I hope you do. I miss the lad, and I want him to square things with Doug." She looked at Jane. "Doug's good for this town, a lot better than some I could mention."

It was a bit cryptic, typical of Mrs Brodie, but it told Jane that she knew a great deal more of what went on in Rowton than she admitted.

"Mrs Brodie, I don't think I can finish this meal, you've given me so much," she said, but one look at that lady's shocked expression, and she obediently ate the lot.

She helped Mrs Brodie clear away and then went upstairs. Once again, she hadn't told a direct lie. Mrs Brodie, like Doug, had just assumed that she was going to Ashburn to meet Kenny, and Jane hadn't corrected her.

But now was the trickiest part of the whole plan. She let fifteen minutes go by, then went downstairs again.

"Just going round to see Cathie Johnson for a while," she called to Mrs Brodie.

"All right, lass. Don't be too late, you'll have packing to do," her landlady said.

"Cheerio just now," Jane left, reflecting that it was the first time that Mrs Brodie had called her 'lass'. Probably as near an endearment as she could get. And just at the time when she was being duped, Jane thought wryly.

Restraining her excitement, she walked to Cathie's as casually and innocently as possible. The girls stayed indoors for about ten minutes, then came out as if going for a casual visit. Cathie carried a plastic shopping bag with two knitting needles sticking out of the top.

They caught a bus into town. Jane watched carefully, but couldn't tell if anyone was following them, but she was taking no chances. Once again, Cathie led her through the back streets and alleys of Rowton until they came to Jones Self-Drive.

The car was parked ready for her in the yard, she had the keys in her pocket. She opened the boot and Cathie put the plastic bag inside, after removing the knitting needles. The bag contained a basic overnight kit for Jane — nightie, toiletries and a few changes of clothing. Then Cathie took an identical plastic bag from her pocket, put the knitting needles in it together with crumpled pages of Rowton's evening newspaper. Now it looked exactly like the one she'd been carrying earlier.

She whispered "Good luck and love to Kenny" and quickly left.

Jane unlocked the car and slipped into the driving seat. She twisted her hair into a bun and put on slightly-tinted glasses to give her a little camouflage. Sunglasses would have been conspicuous, especially now that rain was creeping in with the dusk.

She started the car and headed out of Rowton by a route totally unknown to her, as it was essential that she kept away from places where she might be recognised, even just by chance.

Eventually, by a circuitous route, she hit the main road for Hexham. The rain had settled down to a relentless downpour and she needed every ounce of her concentration to combat the hypnotic effect of the swishing windscreen wipers.

Before she took the slip road onto the motorway, she glanced at her watch. Nine o'clock. Just about now Cathie would be ringing Mrs Brodie's front door bell. If all went according to plan, the conversation should run:

"Jane's been taken ill at our house, Mrs Brodie. Nothing much, just a tummy upset but she's pretty woozy. Mum has put her to bed. You know what my Mum is like, fussy as an old hen. Anyway, we think it best if Jane leaves in the morning straight from our house. I've been sent round to pack her suitcase and take it with me."

If Mrs Brodie's suspicions were not aroused, Cathie would pack Jane's suitcase and take it with her. Next morning Cathie would call on Mrs Brodie and tell her that Jane had gone off on holiday feeling much better.

Jane bitterly regretted the subterfuge, as Mrs Brodie was not involved in this affair, but she couldn't risk anyone finding out where and when she'd really gone. Darkness, as Cathie had pointed out when outlining her plan, was the best 'cover'.

Jane put the scene out of her mind and picked up a little speed on the motorway. By her reckoning she had another sixty miles to go. She planned to stay overnight somewhere as she'd never make Hexham that night, it was too far away. It was tempting to keep driving on and on, but she knew she would tire and if she left it too late, she might not find a bed for the night. And anyway, it would be much better to arrive in Hexham next morning feeling fresh. With luck, she should reach the town by noon . . .

She was fortunate to find shelter in a small inn. Sleep was impossible, however; her mind was too alive, her nerves too jumpy and the endless tattoo of rain on roof and window, the final enemy.

Next morning she breakfasted hurriedly,

paid her bill and inspected the weather from the car park. The sky was pale and watery-looking. Surely not more rain!

The car refused to start. After twenty minutes of vain attempts and several cursory inspections of the engine, she could not find the fault. The landlord of the inn had stood by her, looking concerned but of no help.

"Don't know what goes on under bonnets," he sympathised with her. "I'd best ask Jim down at the garage. Come into the lounge while I give him a ring."

As is the way in some places, time meant nothing, and Jane thought she'd go mad with frustration and impatience before Jim arrived.

"Water on the ignition coil," he pronounced after a professional examination of the car. "All the rain we had last night. Don't worry, I'll have you mobile soon."

Jane bit back fulsome thanks and said simply: "Thanks a lot, I have quite a distance to go this morning."

Jim was as good as his word, but she was almost two hours later in starting out than she'd intended. The sky was now producing intermittent downpours and she found driving difficult.

It was early afternoon when she reached Hexham and the town was packed. She was aware of the beauty of the old town with its fine buildings and quaint street names, but all the time her eyes were searching, scrutinising every man in the hope of finding Kenny.

Eventually she found a space in a car park and set off on foot, making for the station. Every fair-haired man was a potential Kenny, but every time it was a disappointment. As she neared the station, her gaze still sweeping over hurrying figures, a familiar shape jolted her memory. She stopped, puzzled, and once again studied everyone in her range of vision. And then she saw him. Not Kenny, but a tall, heavily-built man, standing in the feet-astride, shoulders-hunched pose of the boxer. It couldn't be Carl Reyburn's assistant, not here!

Hastily, she donned the glasses again. The man had his back to her, so she couldn't positively identify him. She walked a little closer, but the man stood rock-still. She realised she would have to walk right in front of him before she could see his face. That was far too risky. And the only way into the station from here was directly past him.

Abruptly Jane swung round and walked away. It couldn't be him. No-one but Cathie knew she was here. She hurried down the street searching for a telephone box. Of course, there was a queue and she stood, trembling with anxiety and impatience until it was her turn. There was no reply from Cathie's number.

She looked at her watch. It wasn't the time she'd agreed to telephone so it was possible that Cathie had slipped out for shopping, but Jane could have wept.

She left the telephone box and stood outside for a moment, uncertain of her next move. All around her, life was going on as normal for Hexham's citizens. Housewives chattered, discussing the best buy for the Sunday joint, teenagers drifted past, transistors pounding the beat, and a milk float came along the road from the station, its empties rattling cheerfully.

Jane stared at it absent-mindedly, half registering the name 'Mitchell' painted across the front. The very name she'd chosen as her incognito in Rowton. The float drew up at the traffic lights a few feet from her, and she found her gaze resting on the driver. She could see only his profile but suddenly all her senses came instantly alive.

It was Kenny!

She darted forward but at that moment the lights changed to green and the float drove away. Her shouts of "Kenny! Kenny!" were swallowed by the noise of revving engines and rattling bottles.

Horrified she watched the float disappear down the road. The name 'Mitchell' was painted on the tailgate with another name beneath it: 'Bunnsfieldacre'. She dragged a pen and diary from her bag and hastily wrote down both names.

Had the driver been Kenny? Had she found him only to lose him again? She'd only had that one glimpse, of course, and she might be wrong.

As she stared down the road, her eye caught a road sign. The milk float had been heading out of Hexham, obviously back to Bunnsfieldacre, which sounded like a farm.

It was a slim clue but she had to follow it up. Now the rain didn't matter, her tiredness turncoated into energy and she darted back into the telephone box and consulted the directory. She found an entry for 'Mitchell, Bunnsfieldacre Farm'. Her hands trembling a little, she noted the number in her diary. She couldn't ring yet, it might take the float some time to reach the farm.

She found a cafe and ordered a hot meal. Stripped of her wet coat she began to feel warmer, and after a few mouthfuls of a sizzling pizza, her tension eased a little. She hadn't forgotten that frightening figure standing outside Hexham Station, though of course, she could be wrong about him, too. Her imagination had been working overtime for weeks. Besides, how could he have known exactly where to come?

A good half hour elapsed before she rang the farm. A woman answered. With anxious hope, Jane asked for Kenny. There was a long pause.

"Kenny?" the voice was doubtful. Jane's heart sank. It hadn't been him at all.

"I . . . I don't think he's back yet, just hold on, dearie."

Jane almost cried. It had to be her Kenny after all!

Then she heard his voice. A hesitant "hello" came over the line.

"It's me, Kenny. Jane," she said.

"Jane?" his voice was a whisper of disbelief.

"I'm in Hexham. Don't ask questions, just tell me where we can meet?"

"What are you doing in Hexham? How on earth did you know where to find me?"

"No questions now, Kenny. I'll explain when we meet. I have a car, can I come to the farm?"

"No . . . better not. Let me think. Look, there's a village just down the road from here. Bunnsbridge."

"I'll meet you there. I'll find it on the map."

"Are you alone, Jane?"

"Yes, Cathie's at home."

"Is she OK?"

The pips went. "See you in half an hour, Kenny." She hung up.

Within twenty-five minutes she was entering Bunnsbridge village. She parked just at the edge of the village green.

As she stepped out of the car Kenny came towards her. She'd forgotten how tall he was, the ripe colour of his hair, his good strong features, which were now creased with anxiety.

"Jane — "

And to her amazement, her non-demonstrative brother caught her in his arms and hugged her.

"I've been so worried about you, sis."

"Worried about me? I've been going crazy worrying about you."

Briefly she told him how she'd guessed his whereabouts and how lucky she'd been to spot him in the milk float.

"I was going into the station to phone Cathie but couldn't find anywhere to park," he told her.

Jane breathed a silent sigh. At least Kenny wouldn't have been spotted by that man — if it was Carl Reyburn's assistant.

She decided not to mention her fears to Kenny. The important thing was to get him back to Rowton as soon as possible.

"I'm so glad you're here," he hugged her again. "But why have you come?"

"You have to come back to Rowton now," she told him. "Doug won't wait any longer."

He looked away from her. "I can't face him again, Jane."

"Let's find somewhere quiet and we can talk." She looked around and spotted a tea-room across from the green. "Over there, come on."

As they turned away from her car, a police car approached. Involuntarily brother and sister froze, but the car just cruised around the village green then headed for the main road again.

Settled in a quiet corner of the tea-room, Jane asked the one question that was all-important.

"Kenny — the money, do you have it?"

"Most of it. I'm replacing what I've spent."

"Spent?"

"My train ticket here, and odd things I've had to buy."

"Why, Kenny? Why did you take the money?"

Slowly he shook his head. "It's a long story, but before I begin, how did you get involved in this?"

Jane told him why she'd come to Rowton in the first place, and found him gone.

He put his head in his hands. "I remember now — your letter came that morning. I didn't have time to read it. I'm sorry, love, but for me you'd be in Canada and out of this completely."

"Believe me, I'd rather be here. But now, Kenny — the story of that day."

Before he could begin a waitress came and took their order. Jane asked for a pot of tea and a plate of doughnuts — she knew they were Kenny's favourites.

He smiled briefly and then began to talk.

"In the weeks that I've been here, I've had time to work things out. I know now that the story begins long before the day I took the money."

Jane said nothing, but was afraid of what she was going to hear. Had Carl Reyburn's threats been well-founded?

"There's an older mechanic in the garage — " Kenny went on.

"Tom?"

He stared at her. "Yes — does he know who you are?"

"No. Believe it or not, I used the name Mitchell at Speedwell Services. Only Doug, Cathie and Mrs Brodie know that I'm your sister."

"Thank goodness. Anyway, Tom was really good to me when I first started working at Speedwell. He gave me lots of hints about the motor trade, took me to some football matches, and got me another part-time job."

He looked at Jane half-apologetically.

"I wanted to save money quickly. I'd met Cathie and things were great with us. I was going to buy an engagement ring."

"Good. I like her."

Kenny smiled, but only briefly. "Her parents will never agree now."

"Where was this part-time job? At the Pretty Puma?"

He looked aghast. "How do you know about that?"

"Explanations later — just go on now. What did you do there?"

"Security work. You know, keeping an eye on clients to see that they didn't cheat. That was a laugh. Carl Reyburn is the biggest fraud. Anyway, I also helped Big George if anyone required 'bouncing out'."

Big George! Now she had a name for that big boxer type. Was Big George still standing outside Hexham Station? She shut her mind to that.

"And did you buy Cathie's necklace and bracelet from your earnings?"

Slowly Kenny shook his head. "No, from my winnings. I fell right into their trap. I won a lot, then lost a lot."

"How much did you lose?"

"A hundred pounds — the engagement ring money."

"Do you still owe them that money?"

"No, I don't owe them a penny." His face changed. "You don't think I stole Doug's money to pay gambling debts?"

"I haven't known what to think these last weeks, Kenny," she said honestly.

If Kenny didn't owe him money, why was Carl Reyburn threatening her?

"I wouldn't steal from Doug. He was good to me. But I bet he'd love to get his hands on me now. He never forgives anyone, Jane. That's why I'm not coming back until I have every penny of the thousand pounds."

"Why did you take it?"

"I guess you know that Cathie was ill that day. She gave me the safe combination as I was going to bank the money for her. I stayed in the office and planned to have a sandwich for lunch before going to the bank. Then Tom came in and asked me to go to the pub with him for a snack. He was pretty low. His work had been a bit slapdash and he was worried that Doug was going to sack him. I was really sorry for him and since he'd been good to me, I went." He paused, and crumbled a doughnut on his plate.

"I didn't want a drink. I never take one, but Tom insisted. And then I had another." The doughnut was now in a thousand crumbs on his plate.

"OK Kenny, I understand," Jane said softly. "That in itself wasn't terribly wrong, but I guess the drinks went to your head?"

He nodded. "I began to show off. I told Tom I would see that Doug didn't sack him. Doug trusted me, I told him, and to prove it, I blabbed about the combination of the safe. He said I was having him on, that I couldn't be in charge of all that money."

"So you went back to the office and opened the safe?"

"Yes. I took out the cash box, opened it and showed him the money which I was about to take to the bank."

"And what happened then?" Jane

realised she was gripping Kenny's hand.

"And . . . and then the office door opened and in walked Big George."

"From the Puma?"

He nodded. "My head wasn't too thick to prevent me realising that I'd been set up. George muttered something about Carl being very pleased with me. But I knew they were going to take the money and I'd get blamed for it."

"So you ran."

"I charged into Tom and he fell against George, knocking him over. I took them both by surprise. Everybody else was out of the garage so I couldn't get help. I just kept running. I decided the best thing was to go to the police station, but I knew I'd better keep to the back streets and alleys. Tom and George would be after me soon enough. Then I tripped over this old lady's shopping trolley and everything fell out. I had to stop and pack it all for her."

"Did they catch up with you?"

Kenny gave a brief laugh. "No, nothing like that. The old lady gave me quite a lecture. If I hadn't helped her pick up everything, she said, she'd have called the police. She called me a young layabout — a drunken layabout, she could smell the drink on my breath."

"So you didn't go to the police station."

"Could you see the police believing me? I knew Tom and Big George would deny everything, or worse still say they caught me in the act and tried to prevent the theft."

"I think the police might have believed you, Kenny."

He shrugged. "I didn't know where to go, Jane. If I went back to the garage, they would be waiting. I didn't want to involve Cathie, you were too far away . . . "

"But why did you leave Rowton?"

"I just panicked. I had some crazy idea of trying to find Doug and explaining everything. Then I found myself at the station. I thought I could hide for a day or two until he was home, then come back with all the money. But I knew it had to be somewhere that Carl Reyburn couldn't find me. So I took some money from the cash box — after all, part of it was my wages. I hid the box in an old derelict yard beside the station, then bought a ticket for the first train out of Rowton. It was going to Newcastle, but in case someone remembered me at the station, I got off here, at Hexham."

"But you didn't return to Rowton in a few days."

Kenny took another long drink of tea. "When I calmed down I realised how stupid I'd been. It wasn't my money to play around with, Doug would never forgive me. So, I decided I wasn't going to come back until I had every penny I'd taken from the safe."

"That's why you found a job?"

"Yes, at Mr Mitchell's farm. It doesn't pay much, but gradually I'm putting back all the money I've used so far."

"And where is the rest of the money?"

"In an envelope in Mr Mitchell's safe. He doesn't know what it contains, of course. Just thinks it's personal papers."

Jane filled the teapot with hot water and after a moment or so, poured Kenny and herself another cup, doing everything very slowly, giving herself time to think. She knew Kenny had told her the absolute truth, but there were still some things she didn't understand. Why, for instance, did Carl Reyburn still want to get his hands on Kenny? It couldn't be just the money, a thousand pounds wasn't all that much to a gambling club owner. Suddenly that menacing figure waiting outside Hexham station became more real. It *had* to be Big George. If he had traced them to Hexham, how long would it be before he discovered their present whereabouts? She felt panic rising inside her, but she mustn't alarm Kenny. The poor lad had been through enough already.

"Kenny, let's go back to the farm, get the money and leave for Rowton right away. I'll make up the deficit," she said, as cheerfully as possible.

He looked shocked. "Can't do that, Jane. I have the evening's milking to attend to. Besides, Mr Mitchell is away in Durham until tomorrow. I don't have the combination to his safe," he finished wryly.

Quickly she signalled the waitress for the bill, paid it, and led Kenny out of the tea-room.

"What's the hurry, Jane? We can't leave until to-morrow."

"I'm going to find a room for the night. I passed one or two bed and breakfast places on the way here, so I'll go and book one now."

Kenny put his hands on her shoulders. "I'm sorry, sis, I've caused you such a lot of trouble. Still, you've got a good job with Doug."

"I'm not so sure about him, Kenny. This whole thing might have nothing to do with Carl Reyburn. Doug could have set you up; have you thought of that?"

"Doug!" Kenny almost exploded with indignation. "He's as straight as a die."

"Then why didn't he go to the police when he discovered the money was missing? Don't you think that's a bit odd? We both know how hard and unforgiving he is."

Kenny shrugged. "You've got it wrong. Carl Reyburn is behind all this. When I was at the Puma he was always asking me questions about Doug, about our customers, how much money Doug took in every week. He said he was interested in going into partnership with him."

"But Doug hates him."

"I know. I think Reyburn is trying to take over Speedwell Services."

Jane shook her head. "Doug would never let him near the place."

"There's a telephone in the post office, Jane, let's go and phone Cathie. It's pretty public but I just feel we should let her know we'll be home tomorrow."

But there was still no reply from Cathie's number.

Jane frowned. "That's odd. She promised to be the link, and she must be anxious to know what's happening here."

"Her phone could be out of order, the kind of thing that would happen in a situation like this. I'll try and phone her again tonight," Kenny said.

"No! Don't!" Jane cried.

The rain had stopped and the sun was trying to remind them that it was still up in the sky, but Jane felt chilled.

"Don't leave the farm tonight, Kenny." She saw his surprised expression. "I just feel a bit jumpy about this whole thing. I won't be happy until we're safe back in Rowton with the money. Let's not take chances. I'll phone Cathie

243

tonight from where I'm staying."

"It was a million to one chance that you discovered where I was, Jane, how could anyone else?"

She forced a laugh. "I know I'm fussing, just humour me," she kissed his cheek lightly. "Meet me here tomorrow at eleven — and don't forget the money!"

He hugged her again. "You've no idea what a relief it will be to come back to Rowton, to be clear of this money and to see Cathie again. Sleep well, Jane."

She waved to him as he set off on the track to Mitchell's farm. Now he was safely out of the way until she picked him up tomorrow and took him home.

All she had to do now was keep out of sight until tomorrow. She returned to her car, unlocked the door and eased herself into the driving seat. She felt calmer now and began to wonder about the man at Hexham Station. It didn't seem at all possible that it could be Big George. Perhaps she had been imagining things. After all, how could he have known exactly where to come?

With a lighter heart, she fastened her seat belt and took a quick look at her map. Satisfied that she knew the route, she put the key in the ignition and turned it. Nothing happened. Oh no, not again! Once more she tried it, the engine turning over and over, but not firing. The rain had stopped, nothing should be damp now.

As she looked round, wondering if there was a garage in Bunnsbridge, a dark shadow passed across her driving mirror. She jerked round in the driving seat.

Cruising round the village green, coming up behind her, was a large black American car, fins outlined in chrome. The Black Beetle!

Desperately she turned the ignition key yet again and stabbed her foot on the accelerator. Still nothing happened.

Her fingers tore at the seat belt. She had to get out of the car in time to warn Kenny!

8

JANE at last managed to release her
seat belt but found the car door
would not open. In the seconds
she had wasted trying to start the
car again, Big George had stopped
the Black Beetle behind her car, got
out of it and was now leaning against
her door.

She flung herself over to the passenger
seat and somehow got the door unlocked.
As she did so, Carl Reyburn opened it
and stood close to the car, a tight but
triumphant smile on his face.

"No heroics, no shouting, just get
out quietly, without drawing attention
to us," he said.

"Why you — " Jane began furiously,
wondering if she was strong enough to
knock him over if she should suddenly
throw herself at him.

"Or Cathie Johnson suffers even

more," he finished on a note of menace.

Cathie! He couldn't possibly have got hold of her. A sickening sensation of rear swept through Jane. But where had Cathie been when she'd phoned?

Jane flung herself back in the driving seat. She couldn't bear to be near Carl Reyburn. George opened the door and she stepped out.

"Lock the car, George. You can collect it later," Reyburn said.

"You'd better leave it alone," Jane told him. "It's a hired car from Rowton."

Reyburn smiled again. "I am entitled to recover my own property. Jones Self-Drive is mainly owned by me." He paused. "Miss Ross." His falsely benign expression changed. "Get in my car."

Wildly Jane looked round Bunnsbridge village green. Incredibly there was no one in sight. George pushed her and she had no alternative but to get into the ugly black car. She sat in the back, in the corner, as far away from Carl Reyburn as possible.

So, he knew now that she was Kenny's sister and thereby why she'd gone to the Pretty Puma in the first place. But what was this all about?

"You were very clever, Miss Ross. I admire you for that. Unfortunately though, not clever enough. Pity you didn't know of my business interest in Jones Self-Drive," he laughed quietly. "Of course, not many people do. It would hardly do for it to be known before I have gained control of Speedwell Services."

Jane stared at him, but didn't reply. So Kenny was right; Reyburn wanted Doug's garage.

"Leaving last night was a brilliant idea, Miss Ross. In fact, we didn't miss you until morning."

"How did you know where to find me?" Jane could keep quiet no longer. "I didn't give my destination to the hire office."

"Cathie Johnson told us."

Jane gasped.

"It was easy to entice the girl out of her home this morning by the simple expedient of phoning her and saying you'd had an accident. We told her she was wanted at the hospital. We picked her up just round the corner from her house."

"You are evil! Cathie Johnson has nothing to do with all this."

He shrugged. "She was useful. Anyway, she . . . eventually . . . told us you had gone to Hexham. When we discovered you had taken one of our hire cars it was simple to check the registration number, phone the police and ask them to find you in this area." He paused. "I told them you were a runaway daughter."

George laughed nastily.

Jane remembered the police car cruising round Bunnsbridge village green when she and Kenny had just met. She could have wept. It had all been so easy for Reyburn. She'd been trying to discover Kenny's whereabouts for weeks and he'd only had to use some pressure on an innocent girl.

"What have you done to Cathie?"

Carl Reyburn waved his hand dismissively. "Nothing drastic. She gave you away pretty easily."

Jane felt cold. Cathie had shown such resource and determination only yesterday. She would not have given her away 'pretty easily'.

"I told her that I had caught you and was holding you until Kenny Ross was found. She said you were to meet him at Hexham Station," Reyburn went on. "Now. Let's go and visit your brother."

Jane turned and looked helplessly out of the car window. There was nothing she could do. Nothing. Any protest to a passer-by, any cry for help, would be paid for by Cathie. Reyburn had plenty of associates back in Rowton to deal with her.

She waited, all hope gone, for George to start the car and drive up the farm lane which Kenny had taken only a few moments ago.

"Well, we're waiting," Reyburn said impatiently.

Slowly she turned to look at him, puzzled by his words.

"Where is he?" The man's voice was sharp with anger now.

Jane kept her face perfectly controlled but hope was leaping up inside her. They didn't know where Kenny was! They couldn't have seen him make off up the farm lane, they must have been too late in arriving. She'd have to be very careful, though.

She shrugged. "He wasn't at Hexham Station."

"We know that. George waited there for a couple of hours. Why have you come here?"

She looked out of the car window. "I was looking for a place to stay overnight."

Reyburn gripped her shoulder viciously. "Don't lie. You just didn't happen to drive out this side of Hexham. You don't do things without purpose. Don't forget, Miss Ross, I know how you think!"

She hesitated. "All right. Cathie didn't know but we arranged to meet here. He hasn't turned up."

"When were you to meet him?"

"Two hours ago."

"Did he have transport?"

"Yes, a van, he's been working for a dry cl — " she stopped abruptly, as if she'd given away too much.

Carl Reyburn laughed softly. "Poor Miss Ross. Bit of an amateur at this game, aren't you? Dry cleaning firm. Can't be too many of these in this area." He leaned over to speak to George. "Any contacts we can use here to check the cleaners?"

They conversed briefly. Jane slumped in the corner again, managing to look the picture of misery, but inwardly exultant that they believed her fabrication.

"We need somewhere to keep her until he turns up," George said.

"I'd already thought of that," Reyburn

said. "I spotted a caravan site not far away. We'll rent a van for the weekend. Ross will turn up here sooner or later. He'll hang around waiting for her. We'll get him. Now, take that road over there."

For a moment Jane thought Reyburn had pointed to the farm lane, but about fifty yards beyond it was a proper road. George started up the car, swung it round the village green and took the road for the caravan site.

"Keep out of sight," Reyburn instructed as they approached. "Park beyond those trees . . . I'll go and see the site manager myself. I don't want anyone to see her."

Predictably, Reyburn hired a van in the remotest corner of the field, well away from other occupied caravans. George bundled her straight from the car into the van. She saw no one and realised that shouts for help would probably go unheard. So she concentrated on the surroundings. She judged they'd only travelled about a mile and a half from Bunnsbridge, and must be in approximately the same area as Bunnsfieldacre Farm, where Kenny was working. She could see fields beyond the site, but no buildings.

Inside, the caravan was luxurious with many windows. There was a separate bedroom at one end, a dining area in the centre, the walls lined with banquette seats which Jane guessed converted to beds, and a partly sectioned-off kitchen area. Reyburn and George quickly drew all the curtains.

"Sit there," Reyburn pointed to one of the seats behind the narrow dining table. "Give me your handbag."

He rifled through it quickly, then handed George her driving licence.

"Get back to the village. When Ross turns up show him this. That will convince him that we have his sister. He'll come quietly then."

George lumbered out of the caravan and they heard the car starting up a few moments later. Reyburn carefully locked the van door, pocketed the key then came and sat down opposite her.

"What's behind all this?" Jane demanded. "There was only a thousand pounds in the cash box that Kenny took. You see more money than that almost every night in your gambling club."

Reyburn laughed shortly. "Is that all it is — a thousand? So Doug is not doing as well as he makes out. No matter, he's finished now, anyway."

"Finished?"

Reyburn lit a thin black cigar and leaned back in his chair.

"I didn't set this up to steal a pathetic thousand, Miss Ross," he told her. "My aim is to discredit Doug. I planned to tell everyone that Doug Evans told Kenny to steal that money, and then he'd claim the insurance. I had witnesses that Ross took the money and, of course, Doug was conveniently out of town.

"The original plan went slightly awry, but things turned out even better from my point of view. Kenny stole the money. Doug did not report it. He has concealed a crime." He watched Jane closely. "Why? Obviously to further his own ends."

"That's not true — " Jane burst out.

Reyburn inhaled the cigar smoke with pleasure, then exhaled again, watching smoke lazily spiral above their heads.

"But I can say it *is*. I don't have to prove it. Mud sticks. Nobody will trust their car to a garage that has a question hanging over its head, especially one that implies lack of finance. One thing will lead to another. I'll spread more rumours. Clients will withdraw their custom." His mouth set in a grim line.

"I wanted that Prentice Travel Agency contract. I'll get it now. If they don't change to Jones Self-Drive, then I'll get it when I take over Speedwell Services."

"Isn't one car hire company enough for you?" she asked bitterly.

"No. I want complete control of everything. As the Americans would say, 'all the wheels' in Rowton."

"To further your dishonest business practices."

He smiled at her again. "I was prepared to be patient. I got Tom to bring your brother along to my club, let him win some money. All I wanted was some information about Evans' clients. But Kenny was too loyal," he sneered. "But I didn't hurry. I knew I'd find a way. Then it fell right into my lap. Kenny was left with the safe combination. Tom phoned me from the pub as soon as he knew, and the rest was easy. The little binge and then George arriving to witness the Big Steal."

"But all this now, involving Cathie Johnson and me," Jane said. "Why?"

"I'm enjoying this little game. It is teaching you all a lesson for the future. You will *never* meddle in my affairs again, Miss Ross. Not you, your brother, his girlfriend or," he paused, then finished with great satisfaction, "Doug Evans."

Jane flopped back against the cushions, closing her eyes in defeat. If only she had trusted Doug, she and Kenny wouldn't be in this mess now. All along she'd had the impression that he was hiding something from her; it must all have been in her imagination. He'd been waiting for Kenny to return with the money. He had trusted Kenny and trusted her.

If only she'd confided in him, they could have found her brother long before this and had the whole matter straightened out without Carl Reyburn knowing anything. Then no one would have believed the gambler's story. What a fool she'd been. She and Kenny were in real trouble and Doug stood to lose his garage, and that was his whole life.

Now she remembered all the good days they'd had together and realised that then she'd seen the real man — someone who was kind and compassionate. A person she could, and did, care for.

She'd found her love at last, and now she would lose him. He would be ruined and it was all her fault.

There was nothing she could do. Kenny would be caught that evening. Despite her warning, she was sure he would go back to Bunnsbridge and try to telephone Cathie. George would pick him up right away. Kenny would never suspect that anyone would be watching for him. Why hadn't she told him that she thought she'd seen George at Hexham Station? She'd made a complete mess of this whole affair.

It wasn't even as if she could escape to warn Kenny. Reyburn was no fool and she was pretty certain he wouldn't hesitate to injure her and she'd be no help to Kenny then.

Her depression was deep as the evening wore on. Reyburn switched on the television set but she could see he was restless. He was not the type of man to let things drift. Once George returned with Kenny, she was sure they would head for Rowton right away.

George returned just after dark. Alone. He had a muttered conversation with his boss, while Jane wasn't sure whether to feel glad or more worried. Perhaps Kenny hadn't gone to the village, or perhaps he had and spotted George first. He wouldn't know what to do or where to find her, and Cathie was out of action.

George had brought back fish and chips for them and Jane, suddenly restless, offered to set out the plates and make some tea. The caravan was stocked with basic essentials.

The kitchen area was slightly blocked off by a wardrobe which acted as a divider between it and the dining area. The sink, draining board and a worktop ran along the full width of the van. Above them was a pair of broad curtains, indicating a long window.

While she filled the kettle at the sink, she slid her hand between the curtains, parted them and took a quick look outside. It was too dark to see much except a group of trees at the end of the site. Her hand came in contact with the window catch. She grasped it and slowly lifted it. It worked beautifully, no stiffness or tell-tale squeaking. She closed it again carefully. Reyburn might check.

They ate the meal silently and afterwards Jane cleared up. She didn't mind the subservient role, she wanted to keep her mind active now. She must formulate some kind of plan since Kenny was still free.

"As your brother has not appeared, you are our guest for tonight," Reyburn told her when she returned to the dining area. "You may sleep in the bedroom but the door will remain open. I have no doubt that you are resourceful enough to try to escape."

Jane lay on top of the bed. She heard Reyburn and George arrange to keep watch two hours each. She shouldn't have underestimated Reyburn. He would watch her all the time. There was no point in making any plan.

She didn't expect to sleep but she

tried to relax. She dozed once or twice but was awake at dawn listening to the birds singing hallelujah to the new day. The grease from her fried meal tasted rancid in her mouth and she was dying for a cup of tea.

Leaving the bed she stretched slowly. A single light was still burning in the main area of the caravan. George was sitting under it reading a newspaper.

Jane made a few scuffling noises, enough to alert George that she was awake and then she went into the dining section. Reyburn was fast asleep on one of the banquette beds.

She had intended to have a wash and a good brushing session on her hair, but that would have to wait. The only opportunity of escaping would be now, when Reyburn was off guard, but she would have to be as quiet as possible.

"Can I have some tea, I feel awful," she spoke to George in a hoarse whisper.

He looked at her suspiciously for a moment.

"All right," he growled. "Be quiet about it."

She nodded in the direction of the sleeping Reyburn.

"What about him?" she said quietly.

"You can make him a fresh pot when he wakens," George said nastily.

Affecting a cowed attitude, Jane crept into the kitchen. She stepped behind the wardrobe section and looked round. George could not see her. Taking off her shoes she jammed them into her pockets then tip-toed over to the sink unit. She heaved herself onto the draining board. Still keeping a wary eye open for George she turned on the water tap, but let it run slowly. She could not afford to waken Reyburn.

With great care she parted the curtains, grasped the handle and pushed open the window as wide as it would go. Swinging her body round, she stuck her legs out of the window. She rolled over on to her stomach and wriggled her body over the window sill — then let go.

She landed on wet grass, letting her body go slack to prevent jarring her bones and also to make as little noise as possible. She rolled over twice, sat up, jammed her feet into her shoes and looked for cover. The belt of trees lay nearest and she ran towards it. George would soon become suspicious when no tea appeared.

Once in the shelter of the pines, she experienced a sickening disappointment. A quick survey of the site showed her that she was as far away as could be from the entrance road.

She began to run, weaving through the trees, quite sure she'd lost her surprise initiative. Any second now George would come looking for her, but so far no shouts disturbed the birds' harmonising.

The whole caravan site was silent. Jane decided not to waken anyone for help. She had no idea what Reyburn had told the site manager, and her story might not be believed.

She cleared the trees, found the road

and kept running, her eyes darting in all directions. She could see two, three, four fields — all populated by cattle. Which ones belonged to Bunnsfieldacre Farm?

Then she heard a car engine. It had to be Reyburn and George, no one else was up at this hour!

There was a tight bend in the road ahead and she spurted for shelter, diving out of sight behind a ragged hedge. It was while she was regaining her breath that she realised the car was travelling *to* the caravan site — not from it. Maybe she should call for help. Then again, it could be one of Reyburn's associates.

As she hesitated the car screeched round the corner. It was a white Cortina and she clearly saw the occupants; Doug and Alan Nelson! She reached out, calling for Doug but the car engine revved up on the straight and they neither saw nor heard her. Jane clung to the hedge for support, shock making her thoughts whirl. It was obvious the men were making for the caravan site, but how had they known where to come? Her first instinct was to run after them, to warn them about Reyburn and George. But then she thought it would be much better to find Kenny and other help.

She ran on again, round the corner. She saw a farmhouse just a field away and decided to make for it, praying it was Bunnsfieldacre. She reached a group of barns first, inquisitive hens dancing aside as she approached and she almost fell over a bicycle half-propped against a wall.

From inside the last barn a voice called: "Who is it?"

Jane stopped. "I need help," she gasped.

There was a rush of footsteps and suddenly Kenny was by her side.

"Jane! What on earth — "

"Get the police. Now. The caravan site. Reyburn and George. Doug and Alan have just passed me on the way." She bent over to ease her breathing.

"Jane, you must sit down!"

"No time. I'm taking this bicycle." She grabbed the old machine. "Run, Kenny. Now! Reyburn's men are holding Cathie in Rowton!"

As she leapt on to the bicycle she saw the white rage on her brother's face. Then he ran for the farmhouse.

There was a tractor track along the side of the field and she free-wheeled down the slope, hardly aware of what she was doing. There was only one thought in her mind. To get to Doug. To try to save this situation — for him.

She heard the shouts as she reached the site. The Cortina was parked at the manager's office. There was no sign of Reyburn's car, but she could see two men fighting by the side of the luxury caravan. The bicycle took her there in a matter of seconds.

"Doug!" she screamed as George swung a huge fist at him.

Doug dodged the punch and looked round quickly.

"Jane! Are you all right?"

"Look out!" she screamed again as George prepared to take advantage of Doug's inattention.

Once again Doug was too quick for him. Jane was terrified, though. George was a trained boxer. He'd make mincemeat of Doug. She couldn't bear anything to happen to him!

She circled round the fighting pair, trying to find some way to put George out of action.

"Jane! Will you get out of the way!" Doug roared. "Do you think I'm useless?"

Jane stared at him in fury — she'd only been trying to help.

At that moment he felled the boxer.

Jane and Doug stood for a moment, both breathless, both covered in mud, grass and other greenery, each glaring at the other.

Then, with one accord, they stumbled towards each other and fell into an embrace, Jane half-laughing, half-crying, Doug saying: "Jane, my love," over and over again. Then: "Thank

God, you're safe. I've been out of my mind with worry about you."

"I'm sorry, sorry for everything, Doug. I've been such a fool," she cried into his shoulder.

He stroked her hair. "We've both been foolish, not trusting each other, but it's going to be all right now, isn't it?"

She raised her head and after a moment he kissed her long and tenderly.

"Yes," she said eventually.

Suddenly the caravan site was alive with people. Other residents, awakened by the noise, had come to assist.

Alan Nelson was approaching from the trees. Jane saw his face when he recognised her standing there, still in Doug's arms. In that instant she saw knowledge and understanding in his face. He shrugged and gave her a 'good loser' smile and Jane knew he wasn't deeply hurt. They'd had fun together but he certainly hadn't lost his heart to her.

"I'm glad you're safe, Jane," he touched her arm briefly, then turned to Doug. "Reyburn got away, but he won't get far. I'll ask the local force to pick him up."

"Cathie! She's in danger, Doug. Reyburn's got her — " Jane began.

"No, love. She's all right. Reyburn held her in his car for an hour or so until he forced her to tell him where you'd gone. Then he let her go. She had the sense to come straight to me and tell me everything. She was a bit shaken so I told her to stay in my flat. No one can get at her there."

"If anything had happened to her," Jane shuddered.

There was a roar of approaching vehicles and a Land Rover swept into the caravan site, followed by a police car. Kenny jumped out of the Rover and ran straight towards them, his face tight with anxiety.

"It's all over, Kenny, and Cathie is safe," Jane told him instantly.

His face cleared and she saw some of the tenseness leave his body. "Thank God you're both all right."

He'd stopped a few feet from them and Jane could see it was a tremendous effort for him to turn and look at Doug.

"Doug," he began haltingly. "I can never tell you how sorry I am about all this — "

Doug took his arm from Jane's shoulder and walked towards her brother, holding out his hand.

"Everything's turned out fine, now. I'm glad to see you again, Kenny. I was certain you wouldn't let me down."

Kenny looked at Doug for a moment, his expression a mixture of embarrassment and gratitude. Then he too moved forward and took Doug's proferred hand.

"Thanks," he said simply.

A heavily-built man had stepped down from the Land Rover and he came towards Jane.

271

"Hello, you must be Kenny's sister. I'm James Mitchell of Bunnsfieldacre Farm."

"Hello," Jane shook his hand. "I — " she hesitated, not knowing where to begin.

"It's all right," the farmer said. "I arrived home from Durham late last night and Kenny told me everything."

He turned to Doug. "I'm glad you trusted him. I think he's a grand lad. Despite all the worry he's had, not once has he let me down."

At that moment the heavens opened and everyone began to scurry for shelter.

"Come to the farm," Mr Mitchell said. "I think you could all do with a bath and a hot meal."

Jane was aware of Alan Nelson directing the police to take charge of George, then he joined Doug and her in the Cortina while Kenny, in the Land Rover, led them back to Mr Mitchell's farm.

Mrs Mitchell received the clutch

of dirty, muddy, starving guests with great kindness and tactfully asked no questions.

The first matter to be attended to was a telephone call to Cathie at Doug's flat. This, of course, was left to Kenny and he looked a good deal happier when he joined them again. But Jane could see that the past few weeks had left their mark on him. He'd learned a lot about people the hard way, and she knew he'd never be foolish or irresponsible again.

"If I don't phone Mrs Brodie and tell her you're all right, my life won't be worth living," Doug told Jane.

"I feel dreadful about deceiving her the other night, Doug."

"Don't you think she knows you did it for the best?" he smiled and went to the telephone.

"She's preparing the best bedroom for your return," he told her a few moments later. "Well, Kenny will be needing his own room again," he turned to look at her brother. "I don't want you being late for work," he said teasingly to him.

It was as neat a way as any of assuring Kenny that his job was still waiting for him.

However, it wasn't until a few hours later when they were all cleaned and well-fed, that the missing pieces of the story were revealed. Kenny told Doug what happened the day he took the money.

"Most of this is my fault," Doug reassured him at once. "If I hadn't given you and everyone else the impression that I was a hard, unforgiving type, you would have come straight back with the money. I've had to fight so hard for my garage that I suppose I've been a bit suspicious of everyone."

"Did you really think I'd stolen your money?" Kenny asked him.

"When time passed and I still hadn't heard from you, yes, I did think you were guilty," Doug admitted. "Then Jane appeared on the scene and I'm afraid I vented all my anger on her." He smiled ruefully at her. "But she stuck the job with me and was always so absolutely loyal to you, that I began to think there might be more to the matter.

"I'd noticed that Tom kept making sly remarks about you. I've never liked the bloke and only took him on out of pity." Doug paused and looked round at everyone.

"Anyway, I began to wonder if he might be involved in the missing money. I made a few investigations and soon was pretty certain that he was in Reyburn's pay. Reyburn has always been out to get me and I knew he would stop at nothing.

"The more I thought about Reyburn being involved, the more I was convinced that he'd some hold over you, Kenny. I knew you'd been to his club a few times and that he'd probably tried to get at me through you."

"He did," Kenny said. "But I told him nothing."

"I guessed that, and knew it would make him hate me even more. I've always been determined that he would not get Rowton in his corrupt hands." He paused and turned to the young constable.

"Then Alan appeared on the scene. By now I was waiting for Tom to give himself away somehow, so I tried to cover up Kenny's disappearance." He turned to Jane again. "I was really hard on you, Jane, but I hoped it would make you convince Kenny to return before Reyburn discovered where he was."

"But why didn't you tell me about Tom?" she asked.

"Because it hadn't taken me very long to discover that you were doing some detective work on your own. And I was terrified that you'd fall into Reyburn's hands."

"He sent a card to me at Mrs Brodie's."

Doug shook his head. "If only I'd warned you, yesterday and today might never have happened."

"You did try to dissuade me from taking the job at the Pretty Puma."

"Did Reyburn know you were Kenny's sister?" Alan asked.

"No, not while I was working there. He obviously thought I was just another Speedwell employee. But he caught on pretty quickly that I knew all about Kenny and he threatened me. That's when I decided I must fetch Kenny home."

Jane told them how she had deduced that Kenny was working near Hexham and how Cathie had dreamt up the plan for her getaway.

"I offered you one of my cars, Jane. Why on earth did you go to Jones Self-Drive?" Doug asked.

Jane flushed. "I still didn't know whether I could trust you or not, Doug. I knew you were holding something back from me, but I didn't know what. I didn't know you were doing it to protect me."

"Reyburn had been watching Mrs

Brodie's house pretty closely and when you hadn't returned by early morning on the Friday, he guessed you'd gone," Doug told her.

"He told me he phoned Cathie," Jane said.

Doug nodded. "He pretended he was the police and just said that you'd had an accident. Cathie naturally assumed it was a car crash. She was told you were in Rowton Hospital. She left her house immediately and Reyburn was waiting nearby. He caught her and said you were being held prisoner until he found Kenny. Unless she told him where he was, she would never see you again."

"Poor Cathie," Kenny said in a tight voice. "What a thing to do to an innocent girl like that. If I could get my hands on Reyburn — "

"She had no alternative but to tell Reyburn. He let her go," Doug continued. "Warning her that if she went to the police you, my dear Jane, would die."

"But she had the courage to go to you, Doug," Jane said.

He smiled. "I had two visitors yesterday. First, Alan came along in a very aggressive mood."

Alan smiled at the memory. "I demanded to know what had happened to Kenny. If you remember, Jane, Doug had been evasive and you seemed to be protecting him. And at that point, I didn't know you were Kenny's sister."

"I told him everything," Doug said. "That I hadn't gone to the police in the first place when the money went missing because I never gave up hope that Kenny would come back with it. But that I was now really worried about Kenny as I knew Reyburn would be trying to find him.

"Just then, Cathie arrived. When we heard her story, we decided to come to Hexham. We knew that if Reyburn was holding you, Jane, he would have taken you along."

Doug turned to Alan. "I know now that I should have gone to

the police from the beginning. Alan was marvellous. First, he checked the hospitals — no Jane Ross. Then he got your car hire number from Jones, it was flashed to police stations between Rowton and Hexham. Then we set off together."

"When we got to Hexham," Alan took up the tale, "My colleagues told me about another enquiry after your car, a father looking for a runaway daughter. We realised right away that it must be Reyburn, and that he wasn't holding you. We traced you as far as Bunnsbridge and found the abandoned hired car. It seemed a dead end, and it was the middle of the night by now."

"Alan made himself very unpopular by knocking on doors and asking questions," Doug smiled. "But it worked. Several people remembered seeing Reyburn's big car and one person had noticed it taking the road to the caravan site. So we raced there to find — " He turned to Jane with a smile. "Our bird had gone!"

"What will happen to this Reyburn character now?" Mr Mitchell asked.

"If he escapes our net, he'll lie low for a bit," Alan said. "That kind always does, for a couple of years or so. Then he'll turn up somewhere else, new name but same corrupt ways. George will pay the price for Reyburn's crimes. His type never learns."

A few hours later they all said goodbye to the Mitchells.

Kenny had handed Doug the envelope with the money. With his wages from the farmer, the thousand pounds was intact again. In return, Doug gave him the keys of his flat.

"Look after these for me. Go to your Cathie, she's a grand girl."

"Aren't you coming back to Rowton?" Kenny asked.

"No, not yet. Alan, will you take Kenny back in the car Jane rented?"

"Sure, it will be a pleasure," the policeman replied.

Doug drove them all to the village

green where he fixed the car. He handed Jane her meagre overnight bag.

"I'll take you in my car, Jane."

The two cars left Bunnsbridge. Alan headed towards Rowton, but Doug took the opposite route.

"Where are we going?" Jane asked him.

"On a voyage of discovery," he told her mysteriously, then laughed. "To discover each other. We don't know one another very well yet, Jane. If we did, we might have trusted each other and I wouldn't nearly have lost you. We don't need to be back in Rowton until Tuesday. We can take it very slowly."

"It might take more than a weekend to discover all about each other," she smiled.

"I'm hoping it will take a lifetime," Doug said. "But we have to start somewhere, don't we?"

Jane slid down the car seat and laid her head on Doug's shoulder.

The skies were grey, the rain was

battering down again, but suddenly it was the brightest day of her whole life, so far.

THE END

WITH SOMEBODY ELSE
Theresa Charles

Rosamond sets off for Cornwall with Hugo to meet his family, blissfully unaware of the shocks in store for her.

A SUMMER FOR STRANGERS
Claire Hamilton

Because she had lost her job, her flat and she had no money, Tabitha agreed to pose as Adam's future wife although she believed the scheme to be deceitful and cruel.

VILLA OF SINGING WATER
Angela Petron

The disquieting incidents that occurred at the Vatican and the Colosseum did not trouble Jan at first, but then they became increasingly unpleasant and alarming.

DOCTOR NAPIER'S NURSE
Pauline Ash

When cousins Midge and Derry are entered as probationer nurses on the same day but at different hospitals they agree to exchange identities.

A GIRL LIKE JULIE
Louise Ellis

Caroline absolutely adored Hugh Barrington, but then Julie Crane came into their lives. Julie was the kind of girl who attracts men without even trying.

COUNTRY DOCTOR
Paula Lindsay

When Evan Richmond bought a practice in a remote country village he did not realise that a casual encounter would lead to the loss of his heart.

ENCORE
Helga Moray

Craig and Janet realise that their true happiness lies with each other, but it is only under traumatic circumstances that they can be reunited.

NICOLETTE
Ivy Preston

When Grant Alston came back into her life, Nicolette was faced with a dilemma. Should she follow the path of duty or the path of love?

THE GOLDEN PUMA
Margaret Way

Catherine's time was spent looking after her father's Queensland farm. But what life was there without David, who wasn't interested in her?

HOSPITAL BY THE LAKE
Anne Durham

Nurse Marguerite Ingleby was always ready to become personally involved with her patients, to the despair of Brian Field, the Senior Surgical Registrar, who loved her.

VALLEY OF CONFLICT
David Farrell

Isolated in a hostel in the French Alps, Ann Russell sees her fiancé being seduced by a young girl. Then comes the avalanche that imperils their lives.

NURSE'S CHOICE
Peggy Gaddis

A proposal of marriage from the incredibly handsome and wealthy Reagan was enough to upset any girl — and Brooke Martin was no exception.

A DANGEROUS MAN
Anne Goring

Photographer Polly Burton was on safari in Mombasa when she met enigmatic Leon Hammond. But unpredictability was the name of the game where Leon was concerned.

PRECIOUS INHERITANCE
Joan Moules

Karen's new life working for an authoress took her from Sussex to a foreign airstrip and a kidnapping; to a real life adventure as gripping as any in the books she typed.

VISION OF LOVE
Grace Richmond

When Kathy takes over the rundown country kennels she finds Alec Stinton, a local vet, very helpful. But their friendship arouses bitter jealousy and a tragedy seems inevitable.

CRUSADING NURSE
Jane Converse

It was handsome Dr. Corbett who opened Nurse Susan Leighton's eyes and who set her off on a lonely crusade against some powerful enemies and a shattering struggle against the man she loved.

WILD ENCHANTMENT
Christina Green

Rowan's agreeable new boss had a dream of creating a famous perfume using her precious Silverstar, but Rowan's plans were very different.

DESERT ROMANCE
Irene Ord

Sally agrees to take her sister Pam's place as La Chartreuse the dancer, but she finds out there is more to it than dyeing her hair red and looking like her sister.

HEART OF ICE
Marie Sidney

How was January to know that not only would the warmth of the Swiss people thaw out her frozen heart, but that she too would play her part in helping someone to live again?

LUCKY IN LOVE
Margaret Wood

Companion-secretary to wealthy gambler Laura Duxford, who lived in Monaco, seemed to Melanie a fabulous job. Especially as Melanie had already lost her heart to Laura's son, Julian.

NURSE TO PRINCESS JASMINE
Lilian Woodward

Nick's surgeon brother, Tom, performs an operation on an Arabian princess, and she invites Tom, Nick and his fiancé to Omander, where a web of deceit and intrigue closes about them.

THE WAYWARD HEART
Eileen Barry

Disaster-prone Katherine's nickname was "Kate Calamity", but her boss went too far with an outrageous proposal, which because of her latest disaster, she could not refuse.

FOUR WEEKS IN WINTER
Jane Donnelly

Tessa wasn't looking forward to meeting Paul Mellor again — she had made a fool of herself over him once before. But was Orme Jared's solution to her problem likely to be the right one?

SURGERY BY THE SEA
Sheila Douglas

Medical student Meg hadn't really wanted to go and work with a G.P. on the Welsh coast although the job had its compensations. But Owen Roberts was certainly not one of them!

HEAVEN IS HIGH
Anne Hampson

The new heir to the Manor of Marbeck had been found. But it was rather unfortunate that when he arrived unexpectedly he found an uninvited guest, complete with stetson and high boots.

LOVE WILL COME
Sarah Devon

June Baker's boss was not really her idea of her ideal man, but when she went from third typist to boss's secretary overnight she began to change her mind.

ESCAPE TO ROMANCE
Kay Winchester

Oliver and Jean first met on Swale Island. They were both trying to begin their lives afresh, but neither had bargained for complications from the past.

CASTLE IN THE SUN
Cora Mayne

Emma's invalid sister, Kym, needed a warm climate, and Emma jumped at the chance of a job on a Mediterranean island. But Emma soon finds that intrigues and hazards lurk on the sunlit isle.

BEWARE OF LOVE
Kay Winchester

Carol Brampton resumes her nursing career when her family is killed in a car accident. With Dr. Patrick Farrell she begins to pick up the pieces of her life, but is bitterly hurt when insinuations are made about her to Patrick.

DARLING REBEL
Sarah Devon

When Jason Farradale's secretary met with an accident, her glamorous stand-in was quite unable to deal with one problem in particular.

THE PRICE OF PARADISE
Jane Arbor

It was a shock to Fern to meet her estranged husband on an island in the middle of the Indian Ocean, but to discover that her father had engineered it puzzled Fern. What did he hope to achieve?

DOCTOR IN PLASTER
Lisa Cooper

When Dr. Scott Sutcliffe is injured, Nurse Caroline Hurst has to cope with a very demanding private case. But when she realises her exasperating patient has stolen her heart, how can Caroline possibly stay?

A TOUCH OF HONEY
Lucy Gillen

Before she took the job as secretary to author Robert Dean, Cadie had heard how charming he was, but that wasn't her first impression at all.

ROMANTIC LEGACY
Cora Mayne

As kennelmaid to the Armstrongs, Ann Brown, had no idea that she would become the central figure in a web of mystery and intrigue.

THE RELENTLESS TIDE
Jill Murray

Steve Palmer shared Nurse Marie Blane's love of the sea and small boats. Marie's other passion was her step-brother. But when danger threatened who should she turn to — her step-brother or the man who stirred emotions in her heart?

ROMANCE IN NORWAY
Cora Mayne

Nancy Crawford hopes that her visit to Norway will help her to start life again. She certainly finds many surprises there, including unexpected happiness.

UNLOCK MY HEART
Honor Vincent

When Ruth Linton, a young widow with three children, inherits a house in the country, it seems to be the answer to her dreams. But Ruth's problems were only just beginning . . .

SWEET PROMISE
Janet Dailey

Erica had met Rafael in Mexico, where their relationship had been brief but dramatic. Now, over a year later in Texas, she had met him again — and he had the power to wreck her life.

SAFARI ENCOUNTER
Rosemary Carter

Jenny had to accept that she couldn't run her father's game park alone; so she let forceful Joshua Adams virtually take over. But Joshua took over her heart as well!

SHADOW DANCE
Margaret Way

When Carl Danning sent her to interview Richard Kauffman, Alix was far from pleased — but the assignment led her to help Richard repair the situation between him and his ex-wife.

WHITE HIBISCUS
Rosemary Pollock

"A boring English model with dubious morals," was how Count Paul Santana Demajo described Emma. But what about the Count's morals, and who is Marianne?

STARS THROUGH THE MIST
Betty Neels

Secretly in love with Gerard van Doordninck, Deborah should have been thrilled when he asked her to marry him. But he only wanted a wife for practical not romantic reasons.